SHADOW
SUSPECT

A Chase Adams FBI Thriller

Book 2

Patrick Logan

Books by Patrick Logan

Detective Damien Drake

Book 1: Butterfly Kisses

Book 2: Cause of Death

Book 3: Download Murder

Book 4: Skeleton King

Book 5: Human Traffic

Book 6: Drug Lord: Part One

Book 7: Drug Lord: Part Two

Dr. Beckett Campbell, ME

Book 0: Bitter End

Book 1: Organ Donor

Book 2: Injecting Faith

The Haunted Series

Book 1: Shallow Graves

Book 2: The Seventh Ward

Book 3: Seaforth Prison

Book 4: Scarsdale Crematorium

Book 5: Sacred Heard Orphanage

Book 6: Shores of the Marrow

Prologue

"HOW COULD YOU POSSIBLY know what I want? And what makes you think that it's something that I haven't had already?" Chase Adams asked.

The man smiled but didn't offer anything in way of a response.

Chase took a bite of her shawarma, then dabbed at the garlic sauce on her lower lip. The two of them walked side-by-side, heading away from the Lebanese fast-food joint and toward a throng of people that were struggling to force their way into McDonald's.

"I assure you," the man said quietly, out of discretion and not from a lack of confidence, "that not only do I know what you want, but I can deliver."

And then he surprised Chase by reaching for her left wrist. It wasn't a particularly aggressive gesture, and yet what happened next happened so fast that Chase couldn't stop him.

The man held her wrist while he pushed the sleeve of her blouse up to nearly the crook of her elbow with his other hand.

Chase immediately flipped her hand over, bending the man's fingers back, before reversing the position and grabbing his wrist.

"Don't touch—"

But then something happened. Something that happened to Chase before, but only when she came in contact with dead people.

The narrative wasn't as fluid as it had been when she had touched Leah Morgan's cold leg—more like tiny snapshots taken out of context than a full story—but it was shocking enough for her to stop cold.

She was staring down at Leah Morgan's pretty face. The woman's brow was covered in sweat and her mouth was open. Only it wasn't an expression of agony as Chase might have expected given the way they had found her; instead, she saw pure ecstasy. Chase's sweat—or *his*, the man whose eyes she was seeing through—dripped onto her cheek, but Leah paid it no notice. As her face rocked in and out of view, faster now, rhythmically, her ecstasy became more palpable, until she tensed at the moment of climax.

This is where the vision skipped ahead, and the man walked toward the bathroom across the hall, staring at his reflection as he moved. He was admiring his own body, which was lean and muscular and covered in the sheen of sweat. Then he reached down and pulled off the condom with a snap and tossed it into the wastebasket.

Time skipped again, and now he was looking back at Leah's form, Leah who was on her side now, curled up with the bed sheet tucked tightly beneath her chin. He moved to her slowly, trying not to make a sound. For a second, Chase saw his hands extending toward her, before pulling back. Then he started to dress.

Chase let go of the man's wrist and took a step backward. Her shawarma slipped from her hand and exploded in a mess of mayonnaise and shaved beef on the sidewalk.

"Who are you?" she demanded.

Oblivious to what had just happened, to what she had seen, the smile remained etched on the man's face.

And in that moment, witnessing that seemingly harmless grin, Chase *knew*.

She *knew* that this was the man responsible for slitting the throats of all four women, of mutilating their genitals with the beer bottle.

This man, this charming man with the dark hair and handsome face, was a serial killer.

And Chase feared that she was his next victim.

PART I – What's Old is New

Chapter 1

HE CAN'T CATCH ME, she thought. *Nobody can catch me.*

Sweat had begun to soak through her gray T-shirt, creating an unsightly V that ran from her neck all the way down between her breasts. The shorts the FBI had given her were a throwback to the eighties; a thin, coarse material that was too loose in the crotch and too tight in her quads. This caused incredible chafing between her legs, and yet this didn't bother Chase.

In fact, she quite liked the raw sensation as her inner thighs rubbed against each other.

In a world to which she had become numb, it was good to finally feel something.

As she crested a small, grassy hill, another recruit, one greener than even she was, came bounding towards her, heading in the opposite direction.

"Hi, Chase," the blond woman said as she passed her. The salutation was so unexpected, that Chase didn't even offer a response.

She just lowered her head and kept on running.

Most of the recruits did the five-mile loop in around thirty-five or maybe forty minutes.

Chase did it in under thirty.

And this was her second lap.

At the apex of the hill, the worn, dirt trail meandered through several tall trees, something that might have once been considered a forest. But ever since 9/11 and the attacks on the Pentagon, the FBI and DoD had chopped down about a third of the trees, thinning the forest so as to better observe people who might approach. Years ago, it was thought that the FBI training academy in Quantico, Virginia might be a terrorist target. And yet, despite these proactive measures, Chase knew that there were spots that the FBI didn't have eyes on, even within their own small, curtailed forest.

Pumping her legs as hard as she possibly could now, Chase kept her eyes low to avoid unearthed roots that had twisted many an FBI rookie ankle. In the distance, she saw two more recruits, both male this time, approaching in her direction. But while she noticed them, they didn't see her; their eyes were fixed on the ground, their steps light, cautious.

Just before they raised their heads, Chase made an abrupt right and spun around the back of an oak tree.

Clearly unconcerned with their time, the men were talking as they ran, gossiping about something that held no interest to Chase. But what did matter, was that they didn't notice her.

When they had made their way out of sight, down the hill that Chase had just ascended, she looked around. It was an unseasonably warm spring in Virginia, and the budding leaves offered little resistance to the sunlight that poured through the thin canopy above.

Chase closed her eyes and listened to a solitary sparrow chirping in the distance.

A flash of reflective aviator sunglasses, almost comically over-sized fluttered in her brain.

"Please... please, Chase, don't let him take me."

Chase's eyes snapped open, and she discovered that she had been gritting her teeth so tightly that her jaw had started to ache.

She looked down at herself then, if for no other reason but to confirm that she was still present. Her legs were pale, her worn runners covered in dirt. Sweat clung to her forearms as if she was newly molted. With a deep breath, Chase teased up the front of her gray T-shirt.

There was a four-inch scar just above her right hip, a bright pink worm that stood out on her otherwise pale flesh. She ran her fingers over the raised skin, noting how strange it was that the area had no real feeling at all. It was as if the area where she had been shot by Agent Martinez was no longer a part of her. She could feel the wound on her fingertips, the rough, scarred skin, but the pink worm itself was numb.

Dead.

Chase took a deep breath and then started sprinting again, an act so sudden that it surprised even herself. Only she didn't head back toward the worn trail in the direction of the other recruits, or even to complete a second five-mile loop that she had done several times since coming to Quantico more than three months ago. Instead, Chase headed deeper into the forest, weaving her way through the tall oak trees, paying less attention to the even more treacherous ground than she had on the well-worn path. And yet her feet didn't fail her.

And neither did her legs or her lungs.

After looking around furtively, trying to make it seem like she was just running absently through the woods, and seeing nobody, Chase found her spot.

In the thinned-out woods, everything looked the same to Chase. And when she could no longer see the path, and the outline of the gray, squat building that was the FBI training academy was rendered but a shadow illuminated in the bright sun, she could imagine herself elsewhere.

A different place, and perhaps a different time.

Chase shook her head and found the tree that she had marked with a G in honor of her missing sister. And then after another deep breath, she wandered around the other side, and started to clear away partially rotted leaves that had hung around from last fall. With these gone, she began to dig in the earth that was darker, more freshly disturbed, than the dirt surrounding it.

As her fingers wrapped around the black, leather case that she had buried three or four inches below the surface, Chase felt her breathing start to regulate. No, her legs, her lungs, or even her heart hadn't failed her. But as her fingers wrapped around the metal spoon, and her other hand grasped the small baggie with the black snake eating the eyeball emblazoned on it, she realized that none of these things had failed her.

And yet, she *had* failed.

She had failed her sister—she had failed Georgina all those years ago.

Chapter 2

"THIS," CHASE SAID, PLUNKING a finger down on the dossier in front of her. "This is the case I want."

FBI Special Agent Jeremy Stitts raised an eyebrow and looked at her curiously.

"That's the one you want, huh? Who would've thunk it."

Chase ignored the man's sarcasm and turned her eyes back down to the sheets of paper in front of her.

It was a cold case, one that had been opened nearly ten years ago. Missing girls, all between the ages of five and twelve, spread out over the Midwest United States. There were five in total, with a potential sixth that was as of yet still unconfirmed—a new victim every year. Witnesses all reported seeing a maroon-colored van in the vicinity when the girls had gone missing. Then four years ago, all records of the attacks stopped.

None of the girls had ever been found—not a trace, not so much as a hair or a fiber.

Just reading these words brought back a flood of memories that made Chase's heart, which was already racing, double its efforts in her chest.

"Well," Stitts began, scratching at his chin, "That's not really how it works. But I'm sure you know that by now, don't you, Chase?"

Chase sighed and looked around. They were alone in a classroom that typically held fifteen to twenty pupils at any given time, but they weren't sitting at the desks. They were at the main table at the front, which was typically reserved for the lecturer.

Stitts was right, of course; an FBI recruit picking specific cases wasn't how it worked, but Chase wasn't a normal FBI recruit. In fact, this was her second time being recruited, if what had happened with the estranged Agent Chris Martinez could be considered her first foray into the FBI. Maybe it was because of the way she had handled herself during that case, or maybe it was her experience as a Seattle PD Narcotics Officer, or as an NYPD detective, or perhaps even as an NYPD sergeant, as short-lived as that had been, that granted her such privileges, instead of FBI guilt.

Or maybe it was Agent Jeremy Stitts' influence; after all, she had saved his life.

But to Chase Adams, the reasons underlying why she was here didn't matter. She was here; and *that* was the only thing that mattered. This had been her dream, her goal ever since... well, ever since *that* day. Ever since—

"You all right there, Chase?" Stitts asked, eyebrows still raised.

Chase shook her head.

"Yeah, I'm fine. Just thinking about my upcoming psych exam is all," she lied.

"Yeah, someone with sordid sexual desires such as yourself... I'd just quit if I were you."

Chase smirked; she couldn't help it.

Sordid sexual desires...

In truth, however, Chase wasn't worried about the psych exam. The ten thousand or so hours that she had put into playing poker had made her into something of an expert liar. It wasn't something she took pride in, but it wasn't something that she ignored either; it came in handy to lie occasionally, and most of the time she was never called on it.

Except with her husband, Brad, and her son, Felix.

It hadn't worked so well with them, had it?

Chase shook her head, trying to clear her thoughts. The only thing that she was really concerned about was the piss test that she knew she had to take prior to becoming a full-fledged Agent. Everything else had gone smoothly, and she had passed with flying colors: the marksmanship, the cardio, the strength, the puzzles. Everything. But the piss test… that was something she couldn't lie her way out of. But it was also something that she would have to figure out, if she ever wanted to get back out into the field with Agent Stitts.

If she ever wanted to find her sister.

"Is it about Martinez?" Stitts asked suddenly, his tone becoming serious.

Maybe I don't lie that well after all, Chase thought. But then she considered that it wasn't her words or even her facial expressions that had exposed the lie; Agent Jeremy Stitts just had a way about him, a way of using his gut like a sixth sense. It was, after all, Stitts himself who had taught her the importance of instincts and how to use them, how to block out your conscious mind and allow your subconscious, the neurons that had been trained over millions of years of evolution, to notice things that a distracted mind often overlooked.

Chase shook her head; she didn't want to lie to Stitts. In fact, she loathed being anything but brutally honest to one of the few men that she could actually trust.

And yet Chase couldn't tell him the truth.

Instead, she opted for something in between, something that was half-true.

"No, not Martinez, but Brad—Brad and Felix."

Stitts nodded as he ran a hand through his medium length brown hair. It flopped back exactly the way it had been before, something that was a bit of a marvel to Chase. But this wasn't the only thing that was mysterious about the handsome man who was three years her elder. It wasn't his frame; he wasn't a particularly large man, but he wasn't slight either. At about six feet tall, which put him roughly seven inches taller than she, and an athletic 190 pounds, Stitts was average in this respect. And it wasn't his face: he had deep brown eyes that perfectly matched his hair, and pleasant, smooth features that were traditionally handsome.

But he wasn't *overly* handsome.

If Chase were forced to put her finger on it, she might have said that it was his openness that set the man apart. She had first met Jeremy roughly a year ago, back when she had called the FBI in to help find a murderer who was publishing stories about their crimes as e-books, and at that time it was only the second or third interaction she'd had with the Bureau. And it had been unique, to say the least. Chase had always assumed that the FBI was an unfeeling juggernaut and that their members took a systematic, pragmatic approach to solving crimes, who relied as much on computers and analyzing objective data as they did on considering the perpetrator. But to Chase, a profile was just data manifested. And yet, Jeremy Stitts had turned this notion on its head; the man was forthright with his feelings and spoke candidly about the importance of her gut. Chase had initially been skeptical, but in Alaska… something strange had happened in the cold when she had accidentally touched the frozen stiff.

Something that made her stop questioning her gut feeling, to cease doubting her subconscious mind and its ability to unravel paradigms that her conscious brain, distracted as it was with her own addiction and problems at home, failed to decipher or even notice.

Stitts walked over to her and gently laid an arm on her back. Her initial instinct was to pull away from the man, but when he began to gently rub her shoulders, she felt herself leaning into him.

How long has it been since a man touched me this way? she wondered.

"Brad's going through with the divorce?" Stitts asked.

Chase nodded. Not only that, but he was seeking sole custody of her seven-year-old son, Felix. It had been a long time coming, and if back then she had been paying more attention to the signs and signals that now seemed second nature to her, Chase would've seen it a long way off.

After what had happened in Seattle, they had decided as a family to move away, to start fresh. But old habits die hard, and Chase soon felt herself slipping away, falling so deeply entrenched in the cases that she investigated that she *became* the murdered women, the victims, and in the process lost all sense of her own responsibilities, of her duties to her family.

Of her *self.*

She didn't hate Brad for what he was doing—resented him somewhat, sure, but that was only natural.

Chase found herself scratching absently at the inside of her left elbow and forced herself to stop.

No, she didn't hate Brad. If anything, she hated herself.

Chase pulled away from Agent Stitts and straightened.

"I know we don't get to pick our cases," Chase said, reverting to a previous subject. Her eyes drifted down to the open dossier in front of her and she tapped at it absently. "But this case… one day I'll be on this case. You mark my words, Jeremy. I'll be on this case, and then I'll find *her.*"

Chapter 3

"REALLY? I THOUGHT THIS was going to be a multiple-choice type thing," Chase said with a smirk.

The man across from her, Dr. Brent Thompson, also smiled. He was thin, bordering on skinny, with a relatively smooth face, a characteristic that extended up to his bald head. The nameplate on the outside of his office door read Dr. Brent Thompson, Psychiatrist, but everyone knew that he was more than *just* a psychiatrist; Dr. Thompson was the gatekeeper. Get past him, and you got your badge. Moreover, it was common knowledge that you needed at least a biannual visit to Dr. Thompson in order to *keep* your badge.

And yet, the air of pretentiousness that this title should've afforded him was strangely absent. There were no plaques or diplomas on the walls screaming his accolades and credentials. In fact, the only thing on the walls was a picture of what was presumably the man's family: his wife, pretty if on the mousy side, and a daughter who looked to be about eight or nine years old given the missing two front teeth that made up most of her smile.

The picture reminded Chase of something her ex-partner, then NYPD Detective, Damien Drake had told her while investigating the Butterfly Killer. Something about how everything that their killer, psychiatrist Dr. Mark Kruk, showed, including the pictures on his desk, had a purpose. That the person that sat across from him, his legs crossed over one another, was a façade, a fake, a ruse.

Chase thought Drake paranoid, but she was suspicious, nevertheless.

"You have a good sense of humor, Chase. Humor is very helpful for dealing with some of the harsh crimes you will come across."

Chase held her smile, but barely.

What does this man know of atrocities? He's a psychiatrist; all his problems, all the problems he deals with, occur inside people's heads.

But what happened to Georgina... that had been real.

"It's the only thing that keeps me sane, some days," Chase replied.

"That's good, that's good. Look, I'm going to break the ice: I know you've heard all about me, on how my recommendation is what determines if you make it as an Agent or not, but the truth is, I'm just looking out for your best interests. Sounds cliché, I know. But it's true. Some of the things you will see in the field will be the worst that humanity has to offer. Things that might convince you that the person responsible for these crimes was, in fact, inhuman."

Chase watched the man as he first unfolded his legs, then crossed them the other way. She waited for him to continue, but when he didn't, Chase became confused.

Was there a question in there that I missed?

After the silence drew out for nearly thirty seconds, Chase felt compelled to break it.

"I'm sorry, but did you ask a question?"

Chase knew that her comment bordered on rude, but she had long since stopped caring about what people thought of her. Besides, Dr. Thompson had gone through countless Agents during his fifteen years as the FBI head psychiatrist, and a little rudeness wasn't going to sway him in either direction when it came to her.

But instead of being offended, the doctor's smile grew.

"You know how long I have to wait sometimes for the person across from me to break the silence?"

Chase shook her head.

"I had this one guy… we sat here quite literally for nearly fifteen minutes. Can you believe that? Fifteen minutes."

Chase *could* believe it; she could very easily imagine someone in her position so afraid of being judged that they locked up.

So she said as much.

Dr. Thompson chuckled.

"You're quite astute, Chase. Let me ask you something, what do you think the man finally said?"

"Pardon?"

"The man who sat there… after fifteen minutes, do you know what he asked me?"

Chase shrugged.

"I have no idea."

"He asked if he could use the bathroom."

Chase laughed and was again surprised when the cross-legged doctor did the same.

"Let me guess, he didn't make the cut," she offered.

Dr. Thompson shook his head.

"No, he didn't; but it wasn't because of my doing. He simply never came back."

Chase stopped chuckling and raised an eyebrow.

"Really?"

The doctor nodded.

"He asked to use the bathroom, then up and left. Never saw him again."

"Yeah, but would you have passed him? If he came back, I mean."

The doctor interlaced his fingers and rested his hands on his knees, hesitating before replying.

"I can't say — doctor-patient confidentiality. But I'll tell you this much: we can't have a man with extreme IBS out in the field."

Touché, Chase thought. *Now who's the one with the sense of humor?*

"*Har-har.* It wasn't Agent Martinez, was it?"

Chase slipped the comment in as a test, to see if she could get Dr. Thompson's poker face to break.

She was impressed.

The man's expression didn't falter.

"Now, that's an interesting case," Dr. Thompson began. "How do you feel about telling me what you know about Agent Chris Martinez?"

Chapter 4

CHASE SHOOK HER HEAD as she left Dr. Brent Thompson's office.

What the hell just happened?

She had gone in with a game plan, but after less than five minutes of speaking to the man, all bets were off. Everything had gone out the window, and soon Chase started spilling her guts about what happened in Seattle, her time with Tyler Tisdale and how she became addicted to heroin. This had transitioned into her moving to New York City after getting clean with the help of her husband. Next, she found herself talking about how she had thrown herself at another job, as an NYPD detective, about her complicated relationship with the detective Damien Drake, and her meteoric rise to sergeant.

These tales had taken up most of the first hour. Chase didn't want to talk about herself, at least not with this level of granular detail, but from the moment she opened her mouth, she was like a wellspring; unable to stop.

Chase wasn't sure if it was a necessary catharsis — and if the racing heart and the sweat on her brow were any indication, it most definitely wasn't — but the words had just flown out of her mouth like some sort of verbal diarrhea.

By the time she got to talking about her first case, about Agent Chris Martinez, there'd been tears in her eyes.

Only once in her life had Chase felt this vulnerable, and that had been after coming off a weekend bender which had involved injecting an ounce of heroin into the crook of her elbow. When Brad had found her, with puke drying on her cheek and eyes so bloodshot that she could have squeezed them for a transfusion, that was the final straw.

That was when she tried to get clean.

What the hell just happened in there? The question repeated in her brain.

Swallowing hard, Chase hurried down the hallway, wiping the sweat from her brow with the back of her arm.

Did I fuck this up? she wondered. *Did I just fuck this all up after everything I've been through to get here?*

Chase passed one of her colleagues on the way, a much younger recruit whose name she could not recall, and like on the run earlier that morning, she walked by without saying a word. In the back of her mind, Chase knew that the others thought of her as a privileged, crusty bitch, and they had every right to think of her that way, but she didn't care. She was juggling so much right now, trying so hard to keep it together, to pass her tests, to finally become a real FBI agent, that niceties and social graces hadn't taken so much of a backseat as they weren't even on the same bus.

The inside of her arm started to itch furiously, and it was all Chase could do to resist scratching. She knew that her skin was becoming rough again, scarred, that her lesions would soon be impossible to hide in a T-shirt no matter how much cover-up she used. When this happened, Chase would have no choice but to switch to another location on her body.

"There are over one hundred thousand miles of blood vessels in the human body," Tyler Tisdale whispered in her ear as he kissed her neck. *"I don't know of any addict who has used them all."*

Chase shuddered at the thought of the pimp kissing her, at what he had done next, and how willing she been to go along with it provided she got her fix. She had promised herself that never again would she be so beholden to anyone or to anything, but goddammit if she didn't want to shoot up again right there, right inside the FBI training academy. It had only been six hours or so since her last injection, maybe even less, and yet the effects had faded, and the need for more was returning. To Chase, it felt like a migraine slowly building behind her eyes, one that she knew would grow to epic proportions until she feared — legitimately feared — that her eyes would bulge out of her head if she just didn't take a little hit… just a tiny —

A hand came down on her forearm not six inches from where the itching originated, and Chase yelped. She instinctively yanked her arm away and took a defensive posture three feet from her assailant.

"Jesus, Chase, you okay?"

Chase had to blink several times to clear the film that covered her eyes and ascertain that the person before her wasn't a potential rapist, but Jeremy Stitts.

Chase shook her head.

"I'm… I'm… I'm fine," she lied.

Jeremy stared at her.

"What the hell is going on? Why are you so jumpy? You look like you've seen a — "

"A shrink?"

Stitts's face screwed up.

"That bad, huh?"

Chase could only nod.

"Well, I was coming to look for you, actually. The doc called, wants you to come in for your physical."

Chase swallowed hard. This was what she had been dreading. She thought she could fake the psych exam, and although it hadn't gone according to plan, the one thing she definitely couldn't do, was cheat the piss test.

Chase's eyes suddenly went wide, and she pinched the bridge of her nose.

And then she was the one to reach out for Stitts, gently pressing up against his arm.

"I think I need a drink."

She watched his face closely, trying to gauge his reaction. Unlike Dr. Thompson, she *was* able to read Jeremy Stitts. What Chase saw was something akin to compassion.

His upper lip curled.

"Can't it wait? The doc said —"

Chase shook her head and she squeezed the man's bicep.

"This fucking doctor... Dr. Fucking Thompson, you should have heard the shit he was asking me. He knew all about Seattle," she leaned in close and whispered the next sentence. "He knew about Martinez, about Tyler — he knew about *everything*."

Stitts observed her for a good ten seconds before answering.

It had worked; Chase had gambled that Stitts had spoken to Dr. Thompson about her, about Martinez, and judging by his reaction, it appeared he had. And she used this for leverage to get him to do what she wanted.

"Yeah, Dr. Thompson knows everything — it's kinda his job. Let's go for that drink. I think I could use one too."

"What about the physical?"

Stitts shrugged.

"Let me deal with that — we need to drink to the demons that you just exorcised."

Chapter 5

THE BAR WAS SURPRISINGLY busy for a Tuesday in the early afternoon. Given the rather remote location of the FBI training academy, Cooper's Crown was the only bar for miles around. As such, it was often frequented by the higher-ups in the Bureau. Recruits were generally discouraged from attending until the purported epic graduation celebration, but it wasn't as if they were on lockdown. Besides, Chase wasn't a 'normal' recruit.

"I'll have another IPA," Chase said, raising her empty glass to the waitress.

The woman looked over her shoulder at Chase and raised a thin eyebrow.

"DMo's IPA?"

Chase nodded and then turned her attention to Agent Stitts. He was only half done with his own beer but appeared disinterested in ordering another.

"You sure you should be, uhh, you know —"

Chase flipped him the bird.

"Hey, I need a drink. Been a tough day."

Stitts smirked, letting her know that he was only kidding.

"You know, nothing will get you drunker than tequila; it's a scientific fact."

Chase debated ordering shots for a moment, but then decided against it. If Agent Stitts had said Jameson, or maybe even Jack Daniels, she probably would've gone for it. But her stomach couldn't handle tequila.

"No thanks, I'll stick to my IPAs."

Even though they'd been at the bar for over an hour now, neither had said much of substance. Agent Stitts had been uncharacteristically quiet, and fidgety as well.

It wasn't like him, but Chase was too wrapped up in her own problems to start addressing whatever was bothering Stitts.

The waitress returned with a fresh beer, and she downed the first quarter in one gulp.

The beer was delicious, hoppy and citrusy, and the buzz she was getting from it had taken the edge off. Not as much as the heroin buried in the woods would have, but it was too complicated to retrieve.

At least for now, and maybe the foreseeable future, as well.

A little research had revealed that it took at least two days for the metabolites to clear her system if they gave her a piss test, and that was if she was lucky; if they moved on to more advanced techniques, she would be right fucked.

"You can't even tell where you were struck by the fireplace poker," she blurted.

Stitts instinctively rubbed his left temple, feeling his way along a nearly invisible scar.

"Well, I was never going to make a living from my looks, anyway," he said. "You know, I never really thanked you for what you did. I mean, we talked about it, sure, but I don't think I ever thanked you. If it weren't for you, I would've surely died in that house. Either I would have starved to death if Martinez never came back, or more likely he would have returned to slit my throat."

The bluntness of Jeremy Stitts's words threw Chase for a loop, as did his candidness. She felt heat rise in her cheeks, and she tried to distract herself by taking another sip of her beer.

It didn't work.

"Look at the way you take the compliment in stride. What a pro," Stitts joked.

Chase lowered the glass from her mouth and licked the foam from her upper lip.

"You're welcome," Chase said. "And who knew you were so resourceful. Really? Blanks in the microwave? Oh, and before I forget, thanks for not mentioning that Greenhorn Adams didn't even look in the gun to see if it was filled with live rounds."

Chase almost chuckled to herself. Retrospect could do that to you, warp your perspective. At the time, she had been confused as to how she had missed Martinez with three rounds from only about ten feet away, confused and terrified that she would be killed, but now...

Now, she just felt foolish.

"You know," Stitts began, turning his attention to his own beer, which was nearly finished now. "We almost fucking died—Chris tried to kill us both."

Chase sighed.

"I think I'll go for that shot now," she said in a suddenly deadpan voice.

***

"I gotta piss," Chase said. As she rose to her feet, she somehow managed to trip on her own heel and had to slam her hand down on the table to stop from falling.

She giggled, but Stitts didn't even seem to notice.

"Go ahead, break the seal, but you're going to regret it."

Chase shrugged and made her way towards the bathroom, meandering her way through what felt like a throng of people, but she knew couldn't have been more than a dozen patrons. What started out as needing a drink had very quickly transitioned into nearly a dozen by the early evening.

In the back of her mind, Chase was reminded of the last time she had drunk this much, and where that night had landed her: in bed with a serial killer.

Obviously, Stitts was nothing of the sort, and was a gentleman if he was anything, but memories of cheating on Brad were sobering enough that Chase vowed the beer that she had just finished would be her last of the night.

Although the thoughts had brought a sour taste to her mouth, at least the headache that had begun to form had stopped growing, stopped brewing.

That was something.

Chase bumped into her waitress as the woman made her way past her with a tray full of drinks.

"Can I get the bill please," she asked, trying her best not to slur.

The waitress looked at her without stopping.

"Sure thing, hon. Will that be one bill or two?"

"Just one—I'll take it," Chase replied with a smile. She may have saved Agent Stitts's life, and he might owe her, but she had since become aware of the average FBI Agent salary. The job may be prestigious, but the pay was not.

She made more than his monthly wage in a single evening playing online poker.

The waitress nodded, then hurried to her patrons to deliver their drinks. Chase turned back toward the bathroom, identifying the characteristic outline of the woman wearing a skirt on the door and then pushed her way through.

After relieving herself, Chase stared at her reflection in the large mirrors above the sink. She looked tired, tired and drunk. And while she really had no desire to look pretty in this moment, it would be too much of a contradiction to how she felt, she thought it would be appropriate if she at least put on some lipstick. As Chase looked through the contents of her purse for lipstick, pushing several unused tampons off to one side, a woman hurried into the bathroom.

Chase nodded and said hello, but the woman appeared so desperate to relieve herself that she didn't say anything as she hurried past. She took the stall that Chase had just come out of, and Chase was about to say something about how there was no more toilet paper, when the woman pulled down her panties and hiked up her skirt even before the door was fully closed.

Chase smirked as she wondered which was louder: the woman's pee hitting the water in the bowl or her sigh of sheer ecstasy.

Chase finally found her lipstick and started to apply it, noting that it only had a hint of color. Stitts might have been a gentleman, and there was nothing between them that wasn't professional, but she wasn't keen on giving him the wrong impression, either.

He was a friend and that was all—no need for Ruby Red here.

Chase smacked her lips together, and then glanced down at her left forearm.

"Shit," she grumbled. She had sweated so much during the uncomfortable encounter with Dr. Thompson that some of the concealer and cover-up that she had applied to her arm had begun to smudge.

Even though she knew it was likely just her inebriated state, her exhausted mind playing tricks on her, the six or seven small pinpricks on her skin looked as big as boils.

Massive, pulsating sores that people could see from miles away.

Chase found herself shaking her head disapprovingly.

What the fuck are you doing? What the fuck are you doing, Chase Adams?

"Excuse me?"

You need to keep it together—you're going to be an FBI Agent, you're gonna find her. Stitts says you can't pick your cases, but you will get that *one. Not now maybe, not in a—*

"Excuse me?"

Chase came out of her own head and looked around, wondering who was speaking.

A third *'excuse me,'* confirmed that it was the woman who had rushed into the bathroom to pee.

And there was no one else here but Chase.

She popped the lipstick back into her purse and closed it. "Yeah?"

"There's no toilet paper in here," the woman said from behind the closed door. "You think you can hand me some from the other stall? Please?"

Chase smirked as she made her way toward the adjacent stall.

"Yeah, sure, no problem."

Chase was reaching for the toilet paper that dangled nearly to the floor, when a thought occurred to her.

Sick, that's just sick… but it might just work. I'm not sure how, but…

"Sorry, there's no toilet paper left here, either."

"Shit," the woman swore.

"But I've got a clean tampon that you can use? Wipe with it, maybe?" Chase said, pulling it from her purse.

"That'll do," the woman replied, and Chase slid it under the stall and put it in her outstretched hand.

A moment later, the woman emerged and offered Chase a smile.

"Thanks for that. Had this meeting... couldn't leave until they finished. But man... had to pee like you wouldn't believe. A racehorse."

"Oh, I believe it," Chase said with a chuckle. "I *heard* it."

The woman laughed as she washed her hands.

"Thanks again," she said as she left.

The second the woman was out of the bathroom, Chase bolted for her stall.

Chapter 6

"IT'S AWFULLY HOT OUT *there, girls — why don't you come for a ride?" the man in the large aviator sunglasses said. He leaned out the window, moving his head to one side so that cool, air-conditioned air wafted toward them. "I'm just a nice guy trying to help, and you gals are being plain rude."*

Chase tightened her grip, her sweaty fingers pressing into the bare skin on her sister's shoulders.

"That's okay, mister, we'll be fine walking."

As she spoke, Georgina wriggled beneath her, trying to —

Chase groaned and opened her eyes. Her headache had returned in full force, only this wasn't the headache reminding her that she needed her fix.

This was from a night of drinking.

"Shit," she grumbled.

She clucked her tongue; it felt strange, as if it were two sizes too big for her mouth. The sound it made was like a pregnant slug falling from a great height and landing on hot tarmac. This, combined with the fuzzy feeling that coated her mouth, made Chase's stomach lurch.

With great effort, she finally managed to open her eyes. Her mind, which hadn't yet caught on to the fact that she was fully awake, tried to convince her that Agent Chris Martinez was in the room, that he was pointing a gun at her, that he was going to shoot her first for not freeing his sister from Tyler Tisdale.

Chase knew that this couldn't be true — she had seen and felt Chris Martinez's head explode inches from her own face — and yet her heart still skipped a beat at the thought.

She closed her eyes for a moment, but then when the man in the aviator sunglasses, sporting the pale blue overalls flooded her mind, she opened them.

"Nightmares when I'm awake, and reality when I'm sleeping," she muttered to herself.

Her gaze eventually focused on a glass of water sitting on her bedside table. This was indeed the apartment that the Bureau had set her up in, except she didn't remember putting it there. True, Chase didn't remember much of last night, but she knew that she was in no shape to do something that required such... *planning*.

A sound, rustling of fabric, caused her to sit bolt upright and reach for the pistol that she always left on her nightstand.

She grabbed the gun and spun, only to lower it when she saw Agent Stitts sitting in a chair in the corner of the room.

"Jesus Christ, you scared the shit out of me," she gasped. "What the fuck are you doing here?"

"I'm sorry, Chase, I didn't mean to scare you."

Chase shook her head, and then ground her teeth to steel herself against the headache.

"Yeah, fine, I'm just... fuck, I'm hungover, is all."

She started to sit up, but then suddenly became self-conscious and looked down at herself. She was wearing a loose-fitting T-shirt and the pair of boxer briefs.

At least I'm halfway decent, she thought.

But then something terrible occurred to her and the memory of the night she had spent with Agent Martinez suddenly didn't feel so much like a memory as it did a nightmare.

A recurring one.

"Did you... did we..."

Stitts shook his head.

"I just got here. I've been calling you all morning, but I couldn't get a hold of you, so I came by. I knocked six or seven times, then I got spooked and came in to make sure you were alright."

Chase let out a sigh of relief.

Thank God, I didn't sleep with him, she thought.

Chase shrugged off the rest of her sheets and stood, groaning as she stretched her back, and was surprised to discover that some of her hangover had receded. It was as if the adrenaline from the possibility of an intruder had temporarily usurped her dehydration and withdrawal.

"I'll just... I'll just get out of your way, wait in the kitchen or something, while you dress."

Chase reached for the glass of water that Stitts had laid out for her and finished it in three gulps.

"Yeah, that's probably better than just creeping in on me when I'm asleep. What did you call me yesterday? A sexual sadist? Well, mister, maybe you're the one who should worry about their psych exam, and not me."

For the first time since Chase had met the man, FBI Agent Jeremy Stitts blushed.

This, in turn, made Chase smile.

"Why don't you make yourself useful and put on a pot of coffee. My head is killing me," she said. "I'm going to have a long, hot shower."

Jeremy Stitts, now politely standing with his back to her, shook his head.

"There's no time for that. I can make coffee, but if you're going to shower, you better make it super quick."

Chase raised an eyebrow.

"Why? What's going on?"

"The reason why I called so many times, and then knocked on the door, and then broke in, a federal offense by the way, is because your doctor's appointment is in ten minutes. And you need to go, or else you're never going to be approved as my partner. And while Agent Martinez was just a stellar, trustworthy colleague, I'd much prefer to have someone who is—how do I put this politely—well, *alive*. And judging by the look of you, I'd say that you barely—*barely*—fit that bill. So hurry up, have your shower, and let's get the hell out of here."

Chapter 7

THANKFULLY, STITTS MANAGED TO sweet talk the doctor, who Chase was unsurprised to find out was female, into letting her postpone the test for twenty minutes while she had a shower, followed by the hottest cup of coffee that had ever touched her lips.

And now Chase found herself in Stitts's rental car as he sped down the narrow street that led from her apartment complex, which as far as she knew was occupied solely by FBI recruits to the Academy.

He parked his sedan in the closest empty spot to the front doors, and then quickly ushered her from the vehicle.

Chase felt better after her shower and scalding coffee; better, in fact, than she'd felt in days. This was something of a curiosity to her, given the amount of alcohol she'd consumed the night prior, and that it was closing in on thirty hours since her last fix.

She shrugged this off, chalking it up to the fact that she had slept past noon, which was also news that Stitts had taken great pleasure in revealing to her.

"You bring your pass?" Stitts asked.

Chase resisted the urge to look in her purse. That too had been somewhat of a revelation: earlier, she had discovered a swollen tampon—thankfully soaked with urine and not blood—inside in a plastic cup.

Stitts had been in the other room when she had first found it, which was a relief as the man would've only had to see her face to know something was off.

One glimpse of the way her lower lip had quivered, and her entire throat buckled like a mother bird about to regurgitate food and he would have flipped.

Chase couldn't remember exactly where it had come from, only that the urine wasn't hers.

"I forgot it," she said without checking.

Stitts nodded.

"That's all right. I'll let you in. What do you have going on for the rest of the day?"

Chase chewed her lip as they passed through the front doors and slid by two security guards who recognized them. As they moved toward the glass desk and the subway style entrance, she racked her brain.

"I think I'm due in the shooting gallery around three," she said. "I'll have to check my phone, though."

Stitts nodded then spoke briefly to the woman manning the desk, before she slid over something for him to sign.

"Might go for a run later, too, but that's all I got. This is the end of the road, as they say."

As they waited for the woman to tick some boxes, a thought occurred to her.

"What about you? You assigned to any cases right now?"

"Nope," he said with a smirk. "Technically, I'm still on medical leave, but in reality, I'm just waiting for my partner to finish her damn tests."

***

Dr. Nicoletta Brown was indeed a woman. A very attractive woman at that. Tall, with long black hair and porcelain features, Nicoletta had brains and beauty. Which would explain why Stitts and she got along so well.

"I'm sorry I held you up," Chase said.

Dr. Brown looked her up and down before answering.

"I won't be checking for alcohol, so don't you worry about that."

Chase found herself nodding. Evidently, while she *felt* better, she couldn't have *looked* better.

"What are you checking for?" Chase asked.

She hated doctors' offices; she hated everything about them, even before being shot through the hip. Chase hated the smell, the glass jars that were designed in such a way to make you think that you knew what was inside them, but if it wasn't a tongue depressor or cotton swab, then you really had no fucking clue. She hated that stupid plastic maxi pad they pulled over the bed as if just sitting on it would contaminate you. And while this place was less sterile than most, and as such was less offensive, Chase still had a sour taste in her mouth that wasn't from alcohol.

"Just about everything else," Nicoletta said with a smirk of her own. "Now, would you be so kind as to roll up your sleeve? Are you right or left handed?"

"Left," she lied, quickly teasing up her right sleeve.

Dr. Brown proceeded to draw what felt like a quart of blood, leaving Chase lightheaded and asking about a glass of orange juice and a chocolate chip cookie.

She was offered neither.

The doctor did some more tests, this time with leads on her chest, and Chase's eyes wandered about the room. She noticed a bathroom stall near the back, which was only partially blocked by a saloon-style swinging door. Her mind immediately started racing, trying to figure out exactly how she was going to, one, remove the tampon from her purse, and, two, squeeze the urine from it into the plastic container the doctor was likely to give her. All without the woman seeing what she was doing, of course.

Fuck, I can't think straight. Why didn't I just stop at one beer? Two? Six? Why the fuck do I have a tampon soaked in someone else's urine in my purse?

"Is that where I piss in a cup?" she asked, nodding toward the primitive stall.

Dr. Brown finished jotting something down on a sheet of paper and then removed the leads from Chase's chest.

"I'm afraid not; that's just for people who don't like the sight of blood and who I would rather not have puke on my floor."

Chase's mood lifted.

"So, you're not making me squirt in a cup, then?"

"Nope. That's old technology; now we just need a couple of strands of hair and we can test for metabolites of nearly anything."

Chase was suddenly glad that Dr. Brown had already moved the leads from her chest; otherwise, she might have thought that the FBI recruit was having a heart attack.

Chapter 8

CHASE CURSED AS SHE ran, mumbling a long string of obscenities that would've made even the most hardened sailor blush. After Dr. Brown had yanked what felt like a fistful of hair from her head, Chase had left the doctor's office in a daze. She acknowledged Stitts, who had waited for her, but then had shrugged him off with another lame excuse and continued on her way.

Something about being ill from all the blood they'd taken, she thought, but couldn't recall exactly.

Chase made her way out into the afternoon light, and then she started to run.

She had been wearing something comfortable on account of her impending physical, but her outfit was far from running gear. And yet, Chase ran anyways. Even with her purse slung around one shoulder, the strap twisting around her neck like an ultra-thin noose, Chase ran.

As she ran, her mind was flooded with images, an amalgamation of her horrors and fears: a giant syringe puncturing the man in the van, making him beg for his next fix instead of her being naked on a soiled mattress with Tyler Tisdale watching on.

"Fuck, fuck, fuck," the obscenities continued, although far less creative now.

How could I be so stupid? A goddamn piss test? Really?

Ever since the day that Georgina had been taken, seeing her bright blue eyes moist with tears, watching her heart-shaped mouth form those words—*Please, help me, Chase, help me*—Chase had made it her goal to find her sister and the bastard who had taken her. And as time wore on, she realized that joining the FBI was the best way to make that happen.

Now that dream was dashed. If by some chance she managed to pass the psych exam, which at this point she highly doubted, there was simply no way that the heroin metabolites wouldn't show up in her hair follicles. And there was zero chance that the FBI would allow a heroin addict to become an agent.

There was nobody on the running path that meandered around the FBI Training Academy, and Chase found herself accompanied by only the sound of lonely birds chirping, and her own heavy breathing.

It's all over now, she thought. *It's all over. Brad's gone. Felix's gone. My hopes of becoming an FBI agent are dashed. I have nobody, I have nothing.*

It wasn't until Chase made a hard right into the forest and off the worn trail that she realized she had been crying. Tears clouded her vision and streaked her cheeks, and yet she made no effort to wipe them away.

She wasn't a highly emotional person, not overtly anyway, but it felt like she had been crying forever on the inside.

And now it felt good to let it out. As Chase made her way to the familiar oak tree with the large capital *G* engraved in it, let it out she did.

Massive, racking sobs shook her entire being, forcing her to slow first to a jog then to a walk.

Eventually, she found her spot and collapsed into a heap, staring through tear-streaked vision at the disturbed leaves.

Depression rocked her like a wave, a high tide that crushed her entire soul. In her mind, she pictured filling the syringe to the maximum with the boiled powder, then injecting it into her veins.

"Brown sugar makes all your pains go away, baby," Tyler Tisdale had told her.

Tyler was a lot of things, but he wasn't a liar.

The heroin most definitely made the pain go away and, in that moment, with her back pressed up against the oak tree, her face wet with tears, her light fitting blouse soaked with sweat, that was the only thing that Chase Adams wanted.

For the pain to go away.

Permanently.

With one final sob, Chase pushed the leaves aside. And then she started to dig like a desperate marmot for the only thing that would take the pain away.

Chapter 9

"NO, COME ON, PLEASE," Chase mumbled.

She stared at the contents of the black case with abject horror. Horror and fury. She had intended to inject the full load, to make all of her pain go away forever, and while she would accomplish the latter, there was no way to achieve the former: there was only a tiny bit of powder left in the plastic baggie.

Less than a fifth of a gram, she guessed.

And, as with all addicts, the thing that preoccupied her most wasn't so much her next hit, but the fear of not having another hit. And this was a reality that Chase was now facing.

She had brought her dope with her from New York, but that had been more than two months ago. And with her usage rate increasing the closer it got to her exams, it was inevitable that she would run out.

And as Chase started to boil the tiny amount of powder that was left on the spoon, it was evident that time had come.

"Fuck," she spat as she first loaded the syringe, and then pulled her sweatshirt sleeve up past her elbow. This time, she didn't even bother using the alcohol swabs to wipe the area before she drove the needle into her already toughening skin.

As predicted, even after she forced the plunger down as far as it would go, the only thing that she got from the hit was a slight increase in heart rate and dilated pupils.

No euphoria, no sudden gasp. Worst of all, the pain was still there.

As was Georgina, staring at her with her soggy cheeks and small, upturned nose.

"Fuck," Chase said again, only this time it was more like a whisper than an angry curse.

When an addict ran out of dope, the only thing that concerned them was getting more.

***

"I'll be back in an hour, no more, no less."

Stitts stared at her with one eyebrow raised, an expression that Chase was becoming all too familiar with.

"Don't you have your shooting this afternoon?" Stitts asked.

Chase started to shake her head, but then nodded instead.

"Yeah, I do—I mean, I did. But I just have to get out of here."

Stitts didn't say anything, but he didn't immediately relinquish his keys either.

"Where do you need to go?" Stitts asked. "I'll take you there."

Now it was Chase's turn to be suspicious. She couldn't tell if Stitts was just being polite, or if he was trying to babysit her. Either way, Chase had no time for this.

"Jeremy, I just need to get out. I need to get out of here, I need to clear my head."

Chase could see that Stitts was still torn, and she debated laying it on thicker or just letting her words hang in the air.

She opted for the latter.

"Last night…" Stitts said, letting his sentence trail off. Finishing was unnecessary; Chase knew exactly what he was going to say.

"An hour. An hour is all I'm asking for, Stitts. Please."

With a curt nod, Stitts reluctantly handed over the car keys. Chase resisted the urge to snatch them from his hand and sprint to the man's rental, and instead took three deep breaths, took the keys, and offered a wan smile in return.

"Thank you, partner. I owe you one."

Chase was nearly at his car when Stitts hollered after her, causing her to hesitate for only a moment.

"We're not partners until after your test results come back, Chase. Remember that."

Chapter 10

QUANTICO, VIRGINIA WAS PROBABLY one of the safest cities in all of the United States, which didn't come as much of a surprise to Chase, given that the FBI training academy was located there. However, this posed a special problem for Chase; while she was well-versed in the intricacies of drug dealing and pimping, her experience came from Seattle. And Seattle was a far different environment than Quantico. As a result, she found herself having to drive twenty minutes toward Woodbridge before she eventually started to recognize some of the telltale signs of crime and corruption: run-down houses, litter clogging the gutters, people intently staring at every car that passed.

Chase slowed as she drove through some of the sketchier streets, wishing that it was closer to nightfall when her people would be more active.

Drug dealers were notoriously nocturnal folk.

Eventually, Chase pulled up to a curb out front of a dilapidated structure covered in nonsensical graffiti — *The Goat is coming; The Marrow teems with life and death; Mater est, matrem omnium.* It wasn't the house that had drawn her attention, but rather the youths sitting on the cracked concrete steps outside sipping from bottles buried in brown bags. For once, Chase was grateful that her appearance was far from stellar, that she had black circles under her eyes and was fighting the last vestiges of her hangover from drinking with Stitts the night before.

It would help her fit in.

Chase slowly rolled down the window and nodded at one of the youths who simply stared at her before going back to drinking. The reek of pot was thick in the air, which was a good sign. And yet, despite the familiarity of the setting, she felt far from safe.

Why didn't I bring my gun, just in case?

"Hey," she hollered with another head nod to the three youths.

The youngest of the three, a man with sunken eyes and a thin wispy goatee, sneered at her but offered nothing substantial in terms of a response.

Clearly, there was a language divide here. To make sure that they were all speaking the same tongue, Chase reached into her purse and pulled out the universal language.

She held the hundred-dollar bill curled tightly in her fist, exposing only about half its length.

Chase whistled, and wispy goatee turned to look at her again. This time, however, when he saw the bill in her hand, he stood. The man whispered something to one of his friends, and then slowly sauntered across the street, glancing cautiously in both directions as he did.

Chase felt her heart start to race in her chest, and if it weren't for the creeping sensation under her skin, the itching, she would have been inclined to get out of there.

Something just didn't feel right.

"What you want," the man demanded when he was within several feet of the car. He curled his upper lip as he spoke, revealing a gold incisor.

"Brown sugar," Chase replied simply.

The man sucked his teeth.

"You more like white sugar. And *yous* in the wrong part of town. *Why'n't* you git *yer* cracker ass *outta hea* 'fore some bad happen."

Movement behind the man drew Chase's attention. The other youths from the steps had started across the street now.

"I need three gs."

The youth took a large swig from his brown bag, then leaned in close. His eyes were bloodshot and jaundiced, and he reeked like skunk.

"What you need, *issa* git the fuck *outta* here."

Chase turned her hand over and opened her palm, showing just enough of the bill for the man to realize it was a hundred. He tried to pass it off like he didn't care, but his eyes lingered for a moment too long. Chase snapped her fist closed.

"That's a good deal for three g, and you know it. Either you've got it, or you don't. I'm not here to play games."

The man sucked his teeth again and started to reach into his pocket. When his pals appeared at his side, however, he changed his mind and instead grabbed the half-open window, just as Chase pulled her hand and the money back inside. The man's baby finger had a long, thick, yellow nail attached to it that tapped on the glass.

"A good deal is that I take that money from your pretty little hand and if you lucky, I give you some of *dis*."

With that, the thug reached down and grabbed the crotch of his soiled jeans and lifted.

The longer this went on, the more likely something bad was going to happen, Chase knew from experience.

"I've got another one of these in my purse," she said, flicking her eyes to the bag on the passenger seat. She unfurled her hand and held up the hundred. "Take this one, give me the dope, and I'll give you the second one. That's more than fair."

The man wanted to sneer again, but she could literally hear the gears inside his head turning. Two-hundred bucks for three grams of brown sugar that was likely cut with more powder than Sean Patrick Flanery was a ridiculous overpayment and they all knew it.

The man reached for the hundred-dollar bill, but Chase pulled it back.

"Let me see the dope first," she demanded. After a furtive glance at his colleagues, the man reached into his pocket and then pulled out three small plastic bags of brown powder. None of them had the insignia of the snake devouring the eyeball on it that she was familiar with, but Chase could tell just by looking at them, that they were at least the right product. Diluted, cut with God knows a lot, certainly, but it was heroin.

Chase's need for a fix pushed her fear to the back burner.

The exchange was surprisingly quick and uneventful. Chase handed over the bill then slipped the three baggies into her purse. She was about to slip the car into drive and get the hell out of there when a hand suddenly reached through the window and grabbed her roughly around the throat. She gasped and tried to twist away from it, but the grip was too strong.

Her eyes bulged from her head.

"You try to leave without the other hundred, you *lil* white bitch?"

For such a skinny man, his fingers were like iron, and his long nails bit into the soft skin underneath her chin hard enough to draw blood.

"Okay," she croaked. Her mind was racing as she tried to come up with a way to escape while keeping her throat intact, and not parting with another hundred dollars. "Just let go."

She grabbed the man's wrist and tried desperately to peel his hand from her neck.

"No, bitch, you give me the money then maybe I let you go."

Chase tried to nod, but the man must've thought she was trying to get away and only squeezed harder. Her breath had been reduced to an occasional wheeze, and she felt spit coat her bottom lip and chin. With her free hand, she started to reach into her purse and sift through the contents in search of the other hundred bill.

But instead of finding the dry, familiar shape of a rolled-up bill, her hand found something else. Something of similar shape, but larger and wet.

"Okay, I've got it," she managed to croak.

For a split second, the man's grip loosened on her throat. In one swift motion, Chase pulled the urine soaked tampon from her purse while at the same time tugging downward on the man's forearm. Then she swung the tampon.

It was a direct hit, striking the thug vertically across his nose and open mouth.

He growled and pulled back, his nails dragging across Chase's throat hard enough to draw blood.

Breathing heavily, Chase used her free hand to shift Stitts's car into drive and then floored it.

Chapter 11

CHASE FOUND HERSELF RUBBING her throat absently as she drove, staying to the main roads now in case the thugs decided to come after her. She thought the prospect unlikely, given that they looked half drunk and didn't appear to have a car anywhere nearby, but she wasn't taking any chances. She had been in some rough spots back in Seattle, especially when she was undercover, but that had been... well, that had been *close*.

And yet, it had been worth it, too. She found that whenever she stopped massaging the raw skin under her chin, her hand would sneak into her purse and begin to fondle the three baggies within. Depending on how much it was cut, she thought it should last at least a couple of weeks. And that's all Chase needed, really—to just get through the next couple of weeks. Figure out if she could get her job back in New York, maybe not as sergeant—*definitely* not as sergeant, given how things had ended—but maybe as a detective.

Worst-case scenario, she could call up her old friend Damien Drake and see if he could hook her up with a job working at his PI firm.

But none of these prospects interested her; moving backward would mean remembering, and all Chase wanted to do was forget.

It took under fifteen minutes to return to her apartment; she had driven quickly, equally fueled by the shock of what had just happened as the prospect of her next hit.

She parked in the lot, then quickly made her way to the apartment entrance clutching her purse against her chest.

Chase nearly sprinted to her apartment on the third floor, taking the stairs two at a time. Once inside, she made sure to lock the door to keep out worried, or suspicious, FBI Agents. She knew that Stitts needed his car back, and she had promised that she would only be an hour, but Chase was preoccupied with more important things.

It had been a long time since her last fix, and her lucid memories threatened to return like a ticking time bomb.

Chase made herself comfortable on her bed, and then tore into the first package of heroin, almost spilling the brown powder all over her pants. With a curse, she scooped it onto the spoon and started to boil it. Even before she loaded the syringe, let alone injected the caustic substance, her mind started to become free.

Free of memories of the day her sister had been taken, of the horrible things she had done with Tyler and the other men to get her fix.

Free of the killers that she had arrested, free of the memories of those who had escaped, free of Agent Chris Martinez, of sleeping with him, and then killing him. Free of Brad, her husband who she loved so dearly, but couldn't fully commit to while Georgina was still out there, and lastly, free of her son.

I love you, Felix. I love you so much.

Chase loaded the syringe and brought the needle to her skin.

I want to be free of everything.

Chapter 12

"COME ON, GIRLS, GET in the car," the man demanded. He adjusted his sunglasses and then flowed out of the window like some sort of pale pink liquid. When he resolidified on the sidewalk, his face had changed.

"My name's Tyler Tisdale, how y'all doing?" When this new man spoke, his lips quivered like rubber eels frolicking in a bathtub.

Georgina was also there, only she wasn't six years old anymore, she was nearing thirty. Her freckles had coalesced into one yellow blob that covered her face, obscuring her features. Her hair was a ridiculous, almost fluorescent orange color, complete with two pigtails that stood straight on end.

Chase stared with a flaccid expression.

"Take her; take her and go," she said. "I'm just going to stay here and watch. Or maybe I'll run."

As Tyler Tisdale's liquefied form started to envelop Chase's now thirty-year-old sister, she said, "I think I'm gonna run now."

But Chase didn't run right away; instead, she watched as Tyler Tisdale consumed Georgina, who collectively somehow converted into Agent Chris Martinez.

"You like the snake eating the eye?"

Chase shook her head, trying to clear the terrifying vision, but Chris Martinez was still there. And, to make things worse, he was smiling now.

Martinez slowly started to turn, and it was only then that Chase realized he was naked. On his back was a massive snake—a cobra, she thought, but couldn't be certain—devouring an eyeball between his shoulder blades that was so impossibly real that it made her stomach lurch.

Chase focused on that eyeball, and as she did, it actually started to move, and a gasp escaped her.

It locked on her.

As she stared, the eye shrunk to marble size before acquiring a light blue hue that was all too familiar.

It was her son's; it was Felix's eye.

"Felix? You okay, Felix?" She asked in a voice that sounded more like Stitts's than her own.

Agent Martinez's back dissolved until only the blue eye remained. Another materialized out of the darkness, followed by a crop of blond hair and a pale face.

"Mommy? I miss you, Mommy," Felix said in his soft, almost singsong voice.

"I'm here, Felix. I'm right—"

Jeremy Stitts suddenly appeared directly behind Felix, and to Chase's horror, he was holding a gun against the back of her son's head.

"No," Chase shouted, reaching out. "No, it's not—"

But either Jeremy Stitts didn't hear her, or he simply chose to ignore her.

Stitts pulled the trigger, and Felix's head exploded in a red mist.

Chase's stomach lurched again, and this time she couldn't hold down the vomit that filled her throat and then sprayed from her mouth.

Chapter 13

IT DIDN'T WORK.

It didn't *fucking* work.

Chase had no idea why it hadn't worked, only that it hadn't.

The heroin hadn't made her forget. While she couldn't remember the exact details when she opened her eyes, the fact that Chase could remember anything at all told her one simple truth: *it hadn't worked.*

Chase groaned, and as she did, her tongue moved about her mouth. Then she gagged. There was something coating the roof of her mouth, a taste that was nearly indescribable in its filth.

She slowly opened her eyes, which was a considerably more difficult task than usual as a result of her gummy lids.

Chase immediately felt sick to her stomach.

Still-moist chunks of vomit clung to her blouse, coated her chin, and soaked the bed sheet.

Self-pity threatened to overwhelm her in that moment, but she wouldn't allow it. Chase had spent the majority of her life pitying herself for something that happened to someone else: Georgina. Chase hadn't been the one that was taken; she'd run away. She'd run away, because the man had told her to stay still. She'd screamed, because the man had told her to be quiet. The simple truth was that when someone told you to do something, it was because that was what they wanted.

And the man in the van sporting the large aviator sunglasses and terrible overalls wanted Georgina—Georgina and Chase.

But he'd only gotten one of them.

At first it was just the police and Chase's parents, and of course Chase, searching for Georgina, but eventually, the entire town joined in.

They never found anything.

All they had to go on was the description provided by a terrified seven-year-old girl, one who felt so guilty about what had happened to her sister that she started cutting herself at the early age of ten. Eventually, as the years passed, Chase sunk into a deep depression that culminated that fateful day with Tyler Tisdale.

"No," Chase said, but the word was more of a croak than a command. She shifted her weight, and as she did, she felt something sharp on her left arm.

The syringe was still buried in the crook of her elbow.

"No," she repeated, more forcefully this time. As she pulled the syringe from her puckered skin, she realized that she'd only injected half the load.

And that half had made her lose consciousness and vomit. That was the only thing that had saved her life—passing out. Had she injected all of it, she most certainly would've died.

"Chase? Chase, you in there?"

Chase froze; it was Stitts calling to her from outside her apartment.

She closed her eyes and tried to hold her breath like Felix had done on many occasions when he was pretending to be asleep.

Stay completely silent, she told herself. *Stay completely silent and he'll go away.*

The knocking that came next was more forceful, and the knock that followed this a few seconds later sounded heavy enough to almost crack the thin veneer that covered her apartment door.

No, Stitts wouldn't go away—it wasn't like him to just go away.

"Chase? I know you're in there, Chase—I see my car in the parking lot."

Chase moved slowly, fearing that she might be sick again. She dabbed at the blood on her arm with the bed sheet, and then put the syringe back in the case with the other accouterments.

After shoving the black case under the bed, Chase made her way across the bedroom, into the hallway, and toward the front door.

As she neared it, she pictured Agent Stitts on the other side, his medium-length brown hair perfectly coiffed atop his head, his handsome face twisted in an expression of concern.

The knocking that came next was powerful enough to cause the door to bulge in the frame.

"Chase! Chase, open the damn door!"

Chase sighed as she leaned her back against the door and waited for a few seconds before finally answering.

"Go away," she said softly.

The pause that followed made her think that her words had been so quiet that Stitts hadn't picked up on them.

"Please, just go away," she repeated.

"Chase? It's me, it's Stitts. Are you okay?" the man's voice was softer now, less demanding.

Chase tried desperately to come up with the correct answer, the one that would send Stitts on his way.

No, I'm not fine. I'm the furthest thing from fine. I'm fucked-up, Stitts. Fucked-up and I need help.

"Just tired," she lied. "And I think I need to go home."

Another pause.

"Go home? What do you mean, go home?"

"I don't think… I don't think I passed my psych exam," Chase said. "That shit about Martinez…"

She could almost hear Stitts on the other side of the door trying to determine if she were telling the truth, to figure out what was going on with her. Maybe he was silently begging his gut to tell him what to do.

"That's just Dr. Thompson," he said at last. "Everyone feels that way after their psych exam. That's the head shrink's job, to make you feel uncomfortable, make you second-guess yourself."

Chase dropped her chin to her chest.

"I don't think you understand, Stitts. It goes—"

"Fine then," Stitts interrupted, a hint of petulance on his tongue, "Can I at least have my keys back?"

Chase looked about the room, eventually spotting his car keys on a small wooden table not too far from the door.

"Sure," she said, pulling away from the door and reaching for them.

With keys in hand, she unlocked the door, and opened it just a crack, hiding her face from view. She dangled them through the small gap and felt Stitts's fingers brush against hers as he took them from her.

"Come back later, I—" Chase started, but stopped suddenly when Stitts jammed his foot in the door, spreading it another three inches.

"Nice try," the man said, "but I'm not going away that easily."

Chapter 14

"**YOU CAN'T COME IN** here!" Chase shouted.

"To hell I can't," Agent Stitts replied as he pushed through the door. The man outweighed her by a good eighty or ninety pounds, and Chase, even with her feet planted, was no match for him.

Stitts burst into the room, and it was all Chase could do to turn away from him, to hide her scarred arm, the puke drying on her chest, and the scratch marks that suddenly felt as if they had been made by infernal claws on her neck.

"You can't come in," she repeated, only this time the words came out as more of a plea than a command.

A hand came down gently on her shoulder, and Chase instinctively turned into him. Without giving Stitts a glimpse of her face, she fell into his open arms, catching him by surprise. Despite their difference in weight, Stitts almost toppled beneath her.

Chase had done this as a last-ditch effort to hide her face, but the touch of another human being caused her to lose control completely.

"It's okay, it's okay," Stitts said as he embraced her. "Everything's going to be okay, Chase."

As she sobbed, she tried to answer him, to say that no, it wouldn't be okay, that it would never be okay, not until she got Georgina back, but Chase found herself unable to speak.

She was just too exhausted from fighting the memories.

Eventually, Chase had no choice but to pull away from him. And when she did, Stitts finally caught sight of her face and his jaw dropped.

"Jesus Christ, what the fuck happened to you?" he asked, reaching forward again.

Ashamed, Chase turned away, once again showing him her back.

"That's a long story," she said, peering over her shoulder.

"Really? You're going to pull that card? Well, I'm technically on medical leave, remember?" Stitts said, miming looking at his watch. "I've got all the time in the world."

Chase squinted.

"What time is it, anyway?"

This time Stitts actually looked at his watch.

"It's ten-thirty."

Chase started to nod, then stopped herself.

That can't be right, she thought. *I couldn't have gotten back here later than four, four-thirty at the latest.*

And yet, when she'd opened the door to hand Stitts his keys, the sun had been shining.

"You sure? It's really ten-thirty?"

Stitts raised an eyebrow.

"Pretty sure. I mean, I've only got a shitty Timex, but it's been good to me the last six years."

Chase considered for a moment that Stitts might be playing a cruel trick on her but decided against it. Jeremy Stitts was a lot of things, but she had never known the man to be cruel.

Which meant that the only reasonable explanation was that she had passed out in the afternoon and hadn't woken until the following day.

"Jesus Christ," she muttered.

"What? What's wrong?"

Chase lowered her head in shame.

"Nothing. Nothing."

And with that, the conversation came to a standstill. It was clear that Stitts wanted to ask her about her condition, to beg her to tell him what the fuck happened to her, but he was too much of a gentleman for that.

"Give me ten," she said with a sigh. "Let me get cleaned up, and I'll tell you everything."

***

The shower Chase had had after drinking with Stitts had been the hottest of her life. The shower she took now, after almost overdosing on heroin and sleeping for twenty hours straight, made that shower feel like a polar bear swim.

She tried to scrub everything off, the puke, the sweat, the tears, the blood, and the memories; she succeeded with most. But unlike after the drinking session with Stitts, this shower didn't make her feel any better. If anything, it made her feel worse. It was as if her body was already overheating, and the hot water only added to her discomfort.

In that moment, with steam billowing around her, Chase was grateful that she'd already tucked the heroin into the black case and shoved it under the bed. Otherwise…

Chase dressed in something comfortable, loose-fitting slacks and a fresh blouse, and then, with a deep breath, and several minutes of contemplation under her belt, she stepped back into the main living space and confronted Agent Stitts.

"If you want to know what happened, just sit there and listen. Don't say a word until I'm done. Not a word."

Chase hadn't thought her entire plan through, but with no more time at her disposal, no way to stall, she simply gave in to her subconscious, just as Agent Stitts had taught her to do.

Stitts pushed a cup of coffee across the table and nodded.

And then, with her eyes locked on the dark liquid, Chase Adams started to tell her tale.

Chapter 15

"**WHICH BRINGS US TO** this, uh, this *morning*," Chase said.

"And the marks on your neck?" Stitts asked, tilting his head upwards and indicating a scratching gesture at his own throat.

Chase sighed deeply. What had begun as an explanation of why she had come to the door the way she had, had digressed quickly into a tale of her childhood, about Georgina, about Tyler, Martinez, and finally Stitts himself, and what he had told her about the importance of gut feelings.

But Stitts was a smart guy; she had told him a lot but hadn't even broached the subject of why she'd taken his car, where she'd gone, and what had happened to her.

Chase again lowered her gaze, staring at the now empty coffee cup that was clutched between her two small hands.

"I guess, the truth is, I guess I just fucked up, Stitts. Fucked up hard, when it came to the psych exam. And then... and then I just needed to let loose. You know how it is. I borrowed your car and went into town, but not this town, not Quantico, but Woodbridge..." Chase let her sentence trail off.

Stitts was staring at her with a strange expression on his face, one that she couldn't place.

"I was at the wrong bar, at the wrong time," Chase offered as an explanation, hoping that he caught on to what she was alluding to.

Unfortunately, Stitts's expression didn't change.

Chase sighed.

"Look, I got wasted. Really wasted, and things got out of hand," she said, studying Stitts closely as she spoke. "It got a little bit... *rough*."

Stitts blinked forcibly, then shook his head.

"No shit it got rough. I get it, Chase. I do. But your psych exam was two days ago. And we already went to Cooper's Crown for beers…"

Now it was Stitts's turn to trail off.

Chase averted her eyes again.

"Yeah, I know, and I thought it was enough. But… my sister… Georgina… I just keep thinking about her. I think it was that case, the missing girl one? That was like a trigger for me."

Stitts nodded sympathetically.

"Okay, I get it. But you have to be more careful, Chase. Bring me with you next time."

"Bring you with me?"

"I just want you to be safe, Chase."

"Yeah, I get that, thanks. But you're not my protector, Stitts." Chase was surprised by the anger that had started to creep into her voice. Stitts was just being himself, a nice guy, and yet his words seemed to rub her the wrong way. "You don't need to look after me, I'm not your property."

Stitts raised his hands defensively.

"I think you took it the wrong way. I really didn't mean anything—"

His phone, which he had set down beside his coffee cup, started to buzz. His flaccid expression became stern when he saw the number on the screen, and he picked it up.

"I'm sorry, Chase; I've got to take this."

With that, Stitts turned his back to her and answered his phone.

"Agent Stitts here."

Stitts mumbled several *uh-huhs*, then *okay*, and followed this up with, "Yes, Director Hampton. We'll come back to the academy, gather material, then fly out first thing in the morning."

Stitts hung up the phone and slipped it into his pocket. He stayed that way, with his back to Chase, for several moments before slowly turning to face her.

"Chase?"

"Yeah?"

"That was Director Hampton."

All the anger left Chase now.

"So I heard. And?"

"And he's got a case for me… for us. Unless, of course, you don't want me looking out for you anymore, that is."

Chapter 16

"BUT I HAVEN'T... BUT I didn't... I didn't pass my psych test, and the medical eval..." Chase stuttered as she hurried after Stitts, who was making his way toward his car.

"You must've passed," Stitts answered as he pulled open his car door and waited for Chase to do the same with her own. "Otherwise, Hampton wouldn't have asked for you directly."

Chase's eyes narrowed.

What the fuck is going on? What kind of game is he playing?

As if reading her mind, Stitts followed with, "I'm not messing around here, Chase. You want on this case, or don't you?"

"Yes, what about the psych exam and the—"

"Like I said, you must have passed."

Without another word, Stitts lowered himself into the car. Her mind swimming with confusion, Chase jumped into the passenger seat and slammed the door closed.

***

"Three dead in Chicago—they need our help," Director Hampton said as he tossed a file onto the desk in front of him. Chase watched as it slid across and nearly off the other side before Stitts grabbed it.

Her partner clutched it tightly between his fingers but didn't open it.

"All women, all in their early twenties. Stripped naked, duct tape hanging off their mouths, eyes held open with matchsticks. Raped post-mortem with a bottle of some sort."

The man raised his bald head and stared first at Chase, and then his beady eyes traveled over to Stitts.

"I don't want a media shitstorm on this one, I'm still cleaning up the Martinez mess. I want the perp caught, and in chains by the end of the week. No more dead bodies, you got that?"

Chase's eyes veritably bulged. Stitts spoke candidly, but Director Hampton, whom Chase had only met once before during her initial week of orientation, was more deadpan than someone who had recently undergone a full-frontal lobotomy.

Stitts nodded briskly.

"I assume you're medically cleared, that you got your polyps removed or whatever the hell you were suffering from?"

Again, Stitts nodded.

Hampton pressed his lips together in a smug expression.

"I wasn't talking to you," he spat. "Now get out of here, both of you. Your plane leaves in less than two hours."

Stitts turned to leave the room, but Chase just stood there and gaped at Director Hampton, who had suddenly become very interested in a scrap of paper on his desk.

Stitts grabbed her arm just an inch above the painful syringe wound and tugged.

"Let's go," he muttered out of the corner of his mouth.

Eyes still locked on the strange director, Chase allowed herself to be pulled from the office, and then was guided down the hall to a secondary office. She was surprised to see that this one had a nameplate on it that bore agent Jeremy Stitts's name.

Another wave of confusion, this time mixed with nausea, washed over Chase. For what felt like the hundredth time that day, and the millionth time this week, she wondered what in the holy hell was going on.

I passed? How the hell did I pass?

Stitts had to pull her inside the office and away from prying eyes, then quickly closed the door behind her. Without saying a word, he put the folder that Hampton had given him on the table and opened it wide. He put the documents off to one side, before turning his attention to the photographs.

He laid the images of the three victims out in a triangle pattern on his desk.

"You up for this, Chase?" he asked, raising his eyes. "You up for a job?"

Chase averted her eyes, and her gaze found the photographs; she hadn't intended on looking at them, not yet, but she found that once she'd seen them, she couldn't look away. Even though the images were much how Hampton had described—duct tape hanging off pale cheeks, matchsticks holding open milked over eyes—seeing these people, these dead women, and not just hearing about them, was something different.

None of the girls were redheads, probably none of them had ever been—all of them had dark hair—and yet something was triggered inside Chase nonetheless.

Georgina...

"Yeah," Chase replied in a soft voice. "I'm ready. I just need to pack a bag."

She finally managed to tear her eyes away from the photographs and looked up at Stitts.

"You heard the boss, we leave right away for Chicago," he said, eyes narrowing.

Chase nodded.

"Yeah, I'll just go back to the apartment real quick and grab myself a bag, a change of clothes."

Stitts started to pack up the photographs and paperwork, shaking his head as he did.

"No, I know Director Hampton. When he says right away, he means right away. We probably shouldn't have come here. I just had to see that you could handle this."

On any other occasion, Chase might have shot back a scathing remark, but her mind was preoccupied with images of the black case that she'd shoved beneath her bed.

I have to go back in case someone finds it.

But that was a lie.

She had to get back because she *needed* it.

"Five minutes, Stitts. All I need is five minutes."

Stitts sidled up next to her. When he reached for her arm, Chase moved toward the door.

"Five minutes," she repeated, realizing how similar this scenario was playing out compared to yesterday.

One hour, Stitts. Please. I just need the car for one hour.

This time, however, Stitts was having none of it. Desperate, Chase reached for the door handle, but before she could turn it, Stitts's hand came down on top of hers.

"Chase, we gotta go; we have to go now."

Rage suddenly overwhelmed her and she shook Stitts's hand away.

"Really? What, I don't even get a change of clothes? Let me guess, you'll have a fucking red coat waiting for me when I get to Chicago. A gun? Sure, I can borrow a gun filled with blanks and a phony badge. Who the fuck are you, anyway? Agent Jeremy Fucking Martinez? What's your problem—"

For the first time since she had met the man, something akin to anger flashed over his face and Chase fell silent. For the briefest moment, she thought that he was going to strike her and recoiled in anticipation.

But he didn't.

Instead, he strode over to the other side of his desk and yanked the drawer open so hard that it almost fell to the floor. He reached inside, grabbed a hard case and a small, leather folio, and tossed both on the desk.

"That's your gun," he said, his lips pressed together tightly. "And that's your badge. Your psych results came in this morning, as did your medical. Congratulations, FBI Special Agent Chase Adams. Welcome to the fucking team."

Chase stood there, paralyzed, one hand outstretched towards the door, the other toward her badge.

I passed... how in the world is that possible?

She must've flinched then, because Stitts leveled his eyes at her and spoke in an even voice.

"If you go out that door, Chase, if you make any attempt to go back to your apartment, I'll make sure that you never ever pick up this badge or gun."

PART II – Duct Tape and Matchsticks

ONE WEEK AGO

Chapter 17

"TELL ME... TELL ME you're not going to do that voodoo thing again, Chase?" Jeremy Stitts said with a dramatic eyeroll. "Please."

Chase hushed her partner with a wave of her hand.

"You told me to use my gut," she said quietly out of the corner of her mouth as she leaned over the bed.

"Nobody's touched her or moved anything. I was given specific instructions not to—"

Stitts stepped toward the uniformed officer, moving between him and Chase.

Then he waved his hand surreptitiously behind his back, and Chase smirked.

Snide comment or not, a fourth murder had occurred while they had been in the air. Director Hampton had said no more bodies, and they needed all the help they could get.

"Yes, I understand Officer…"

"Kent. Peter Kent."

"Yes, Officer Kent, I understand. But you see, my partner and I have been called in…"

Chase let Stitts's conversation fade into the background as she observed the corpse. She didn't know anything about her, only that she was their killer's fourth victim. Chase could have asked for more, for her age, occupation, time of death, but she didn't.

She preferred it this way.

She preferred to be unbiased.

Just her name, all she needed was her name. And she had that: *Leah Morgan.*

The girl was young, and like the other three victims, she had dark, almost black hair. There was a thick strip of duct tape hanging from one cheek, clearly having been pulled back after she was either dead or was no longer able to scream.

Her eyes were open, her gaze blank. Two wooden matchsticks had been placed on each lid, holding them open.

Chase's own eyes, a deep green, moved down from the woman's pale lips to her chin, then to her throat.

Like the others, it had been cut with something jagged, leaving hunks of flesh dangling just below her chin. The blood had soaked the mattress so fully around her head that it was slightly sunken.

Leah's body was splayed out almost artfully, her naked flesh leaving nothing to the imagination. As far as Chase could tell, her clothes weren't in the room.

A trophy… he takes their clothes as a trophy.

Chase inadvertently found herself shaking her head as she raised her gaze again.

"Your eyes are open, you poor thing, now tell me what you saw."

As she whispered, Chase lowered her hand and laid it gently on the girl's bare forearm.

And she was instantly transported into a different world.

Chapter 18

LEAH GIGGLED AS SHE stumbled, wrapping her arms around the man at her side. He laughed too, and put his right arm around her waist, squeezing her tightly. She liked his touch, it felt good. He was handsome, handsome and charming, everything that she wanted on a Saturday night.

"I'm on the second floor," Leah said softly as she struggled to remove her keys from her pocket. The key ring kept slipping in her hand, and the man gently took it from her.

"I'll get it."

And with that, the man opened the door and led them both inside.

They had barely crossed the threshold before Leah reached for him, wrapping her arms around his neck and pulling his head down to meet hers. His kisses were gentle at first, but she forced him to be more hungry, first by running her tongue across his lips, before using it to pry them open.

He smells good—he smells so damn good, she thought as she kissed him.

He pulled away then and looked down at her.

"No, not here. Which room is yours?"

Leah pouted, but then waved her arm towards the stairway off to the right.

"Up there; my room's up there."

"Then let's go," the man said with a smile.

***

Chase blinked and pulled her hand back. Her breathing was ragged now, and her heart was racing.

I need more, she thought. *I need you to tell me more, Leah.*

With a deep breath, she reached out and touched Leah's cold flesh one more time.

***

Leah rolled onto her side, tucking the blanket beneath her chin with both hands. She watched the man's bare backside as he walked towards the bathroom.

Her body was still thrumming, every muscle, even those in her toes, fatigued from being clenched in ecstasy.

She heard a snap, and then watched as he spread his legs slightly and started to urinate.

I needed that, she thought. Oh, God, I needed that to take my mind off… things.

With a sigh, Leah rolled the other way, pulled her knees up to her chest, and let the final wave of her orgasm coupled with the numbing sensation of the alcohol guide her gently into sleep.

Chapter 19

CHASE GASPED AND REMOVED her hand from Leah Morgan's forearm. Stitts reached for her then, but she didn't feel like being touched, and pulled away.

"Chase, you okay?" he asked, concern in his voice.

Even though Chase had explained in great detail what had happened in Alaska with the two girls, about how she was able to piece together their last moments by simply touching their bodies, this was his first time seeing it in person.

And seeing was believing, as they say.

Chase swallowed hard and nodded.

"I'll be—" *fine,* she was going to say before Officer Kent interrupted her.

"Ma'am, are you going to be sick? Because—"

Chase leered at the uniform.

"Ma'am? Am I a goddamn lunch lady? It's Agent Adams," she snapped.

The man straightened.

"Sorry. Agent Adams, are you—"

Again, Chase cut him off.

"I'm fine," she said, and then turned to Stitts. "Let's get out of here."

Stitts raised an eyebrow and glanced briefly around the room.

"You sure? We only just got here."

Chase, whose throat suddenly felt very dry, swallowed audibly. He was right of course, they *had* only just gotten here. In fact, they had only just landed in Chicago when the fourth victim was identified and had come straight from the airport. And yet, Chase thought that she had already gathered all of the information she could from this scene.

"Yeah, I'm sure. Let's head back to the precinct."

Stitts's eyebrows knitted and it looked for a moment like the man would object. But he bit his tongue. After what had happened with Agent Martinez, how Chase had saved him by following these instincts, Stitts had no choice but to trust her gut feelings. And Chase, to her surprise, was beginning to trust them too.

What had Stitts said all those months ago? Chase wondered as she struggled to recall. *Millions of years of evolution have honed your gut to pick up on things that your busy mind and easily distracted eyes don't. Trust your gut, and not only just when it's telling you it's time to eat.*

Something like that, anyway.

Eventually, Stitts nodded, and they moved toward the door. Officer Kent stepped out of their way but looked none too pleased about them leaving so soon after they'd arrived.

Stitts was already on the second stair, when Chase turned back one final time.

There, slung over the edge of the garbage in the bathroom, was a used condom.

That was the snap before the man sprung a leak, Chase thought, *one of the last sounds that Leah Morgan ever heard.*

***

Chicago PD Detective Bert Marsh allowed them to set up shop inside his office, which was considerably larger than the one he commandeered from a lesser detective who was on leave. He struck Chase as a nice enough guy, if a little stuck in his ways, hardened by the job. But he was definitely no asshole, at least not on the level of Police Chief Downs from Alaska. Tall, gray, with military-style hair, and heavily muscled, the man stood at least three inches taller than Stitts, who was no slouch. He was wearing a striped collared shirt and a navy blue tie. Even though this was their first meeting, Chase got the impression that if she stayed more than a few days, she would become familiar with that shirt and tie combo.

Very familiar.

Stitts was on a first name basis with the man, but unlike Agent Martinez and his relationships, their interactions appeared not to have transcended the professional. Chase highly doubted that she would be invited to any after-work drinks with these two.

Which was fine by her.

And yet, as they stood around Marsh's desk, Chase found herself spending as much time studying the two of them as she did photographs of the victims.

Relax, Chase. This isn't Martinez and Downs. You're safe here.

"I'd say this was good timing, but that just sounds plain wrong," Detective Marsh said. He straightened Leah Morgan's photograph so that it was in line with the others. "He's speeding up."

Chase followed the man's fingers and concentrated on the images.

Director Hampton had been right; in some respects, they were the same. All four women had the same dark hair, the same pale features, matchsticks propping their eyes open, and duct tape hanging loosely off one cheek.

Except they *weren't* the same; they were different, Chase knew this because she had spent time as Leah Morgan, inside her head. She wasn't just a photograph of a victim, but a woman.

Agent Stitts pointed at the first photograph, the victim labeled as Bernice Wilson.

"Two months ago," he said, before shifting his finger to the next photo. "Meg Docker, a month after that."

Chase followed along with the time line that she already knew, trying to piece this information together with the things that she had "seen" when her hand had come down on Leah's forearm.

She remembered the man sauntering to the bathroom after making love to Leah. He had seemed anything but hurried.

Chase wondered briefly if she could go to the morgue to see the other three girls but decided to hold back. Detective Marsh might not be an asshole, but he was definitely of the old guard.

Stitts moved to the next photo in the sequence.

"Three weeks after Meg, Kirsty Buchanan, and then just three days after Kirsty, we have Leah."

"He's speeding up," Detective Marsh repeated. Although it had never been explicitly stated, at least not to Chase, it appeared as if Detective Marsh had reached out to the FBI, and quite possibly Stitts himself, for help. And this was likely the reason why.

A month, three weeks, then three days.

"Which means he's becoming more confident," Stitts said, shaking his head. "The first kills, even though they aren't sloppy like first kills usually are, are spread out. Then, when the killer doesn't get caught, he gains confidence. Thinks he'll *never* get caught."

"Yeah, that's what it—"

Chase shook her head.

"No, he's not become more confident; he's getting hornier."

Both men in the room turned and looked at her as if she had grown a new head. Detective Marsh seemed particularly shocked by her words, more evidence that he grew up in the eighties, and was only now living in the nineties. A woman couldn't say horny; no way. Not a *professional* woman, anyway. And yet he said nothing; instead, it was Stitts who spoke up.

"Hornier?"

"What the hell are you talking about?" Detective Marsh finally piped in. His eyes drifted over to Agent Stitts. "What's she talking about?"

Stitts shrugged.

"Chase?"

Chase took a deep breath and chose her next words carefully. She knew that both men were inspecting her and she had to be cautious with what she recounted from when she was behind Leah's eyes.

"I think we're looking for a guy—"

"I don't need to be an FBI profiler to know that," Detective Marsh snapped.

Stitts silenced him with a raised finger.

"An opportunist of sorts," Chase said, reverting to what she had seen. "I dunno… it just doesn't seem like this was planned. I think we're looking for a handsome guy, someone who targeted these girls not because of specific features, but because this is simply his *type*. I think he slept with Leah, slept with all of them, but it was consensual."

Detective Marsh looked dubious.

"So what? You read the file; we know that the first three girls had intercourse shortly before they were killed. And we know based on the bleeding patterns, that the raping with the bottles almost certainly occurred post-mortem."

Stitts stared at Chase as Detective Marsh spoke, and something passed between them. Stitts knew that Chase hadn't read the file, had deliberately *avoided* reading the file, in fact, and yet he implied with a look that they should keep this close to their chest.

Detective Bert Marsh wasn't an asshole *now*, but that didn't mean that he couldn't become one in short notice. And judging by the way his face was starting to turn red…

"Yeah, definitely opportunist," Stitts said quickly. "Our unsub probably picked up these girls from a bar, got them drunk, and then, maybe with the help of some modern chemistry, had their way with them."

Chase shook her head—something didn't seem right about Stitts's scenario—but before she could reply, Marsh spoke up.

"I just got a call this morning; it looks like there were opioid metabolites in Bernice's blood. Coroner says that based on their concentration, she must have consumed, or injected, something very close to her time of death."

Chase gaped.

Heroin…

"There's more," Marsh continued, "it looks like Bernice and Meg both attended an in-treatment program for heroin addiction a couple of months back. I'm still looking into the other two victims, but the treatment centers keep information about their patients locked up tight. The coroner is screening Meg, Kirsty, and Leah's blood for opioid metabolites as we speak. Could be nothing or could be something."

Chase was barely listening to the man; she was remembering the baggies in the black case shoved beneath her bed back in Quantico.

What if someone goes in there? she wondered. *What if someone finds them? And where can I get some more if they do?*

Chapter 20

"WHAT DO YOU THINK, Chase?"

After what happened in Woodbridge, how the hell am I going —

A hand came down on her shoulder and she jumped.

"You okay?" Stitts asked, his eyebrows knitted in concern.

Chase shrugged him off and then scratched absently at her arm.

"Sorry, just tired," she grumbled, and then cleared her throat. "Even if they find heroin in all of the girls' systems, I doubt that he gave it to them. I mean, it doesn't make sense. This guy's handsome, charming... he picked these girls up at the bar. He didn't need to drug them... or kill them for that matter."

Chase realized that she was rambling, speaking her thoughts out loud, but the thought of heroin had suddenly made her tongue come unhinged.

"Something's just not adding up."

"He got what he wanted?" Detective Marsh said in a strangled tone. "He's a fucking psycho killer, and what he wanted was to kill these girls."

Again, Chase found herself pawing at the sleeve of her blouse.

"I don't know... normally, a person who commits this kind of crime does it because he *has* to."

"Has to?" Detective Marsh asked. "What do you mean, *has to?*"

Stitts gave Chase another strange look and interjected before things got heated.

More heated.

"What my partner's saying, is that usually in crimes like these... crimes of such violence, the perpetrator is someone who had no chance with these girls, someone who had to drug them just to get them to look at him. That's usually the MO. In this case, we're looking for a good-looking guy, someone who likely doesn't need to do anything other than smile and bat his eyelashes to get these girls to come over to him."

Detective Marsh frowned.

"You guys keep saying that we're looking for a handsome guy. But why? How do you know that our guy isn't a fucking troll who had to get Leah, Bernice, Meg, and Kirsty so high that they didn't know what was going on before he dragged them home with him? Maybe, just maybe, when the time came to it, he couldn't get his rocks off and decided to get his jollies in a more *visceral* way, hmm? Did you ever think of that?"

Chase shook her head more violently this time.

"I saw—"

Stitts grabbed her arm again and offered her a serious look. Still staring at her, he reached out and pointed at the casefile on the desk.

"Because of your notes, Bert. It says right here," he tapped absently. "Three people saw Bernice leaving the club with a guy, and two others saw Meg entering her apartment with an unknown male. If—*if* he was a troll, someone would have noticed. Somebody would have said, *hey that girl is way out of his league* or, *hey can you believe that guy is going to hook-up with her?*"

Smooth, Stitts. Very smooth.

Marsh suddenly broke into a grin, one that didn't sit well with Chase.

"Yeah, but there's one problem with your theory, with this idea that he just picked them up because he liked their figure."

"And what's that?" Chase asked, feeling her own backbone start to stiffen.

"Our guy never took them back to his house—he went to *their* house."

"So?"

"So," Marsh began, "he must have known that they lived alone, that no one was visiting, that they didn't have a feral dog. To me, it looks like he did a little research before going out, doesn't it?"

For once, Chase didn't have a response.

Could it be a coincidence? Chance, maybe?

Something else occurred to her, something that she decided to keep to herself for the time being.

Where did he keep the matches? The tape? Did he go to the club with a fucking fanny pack? I bet no one noticed the handsome guy with a goddamn fanny pack in a club.

"You might be onto something," Stitts said in an almost remorseful tone.

Detective Marsh grunted an affirmative.

"Why their houses at all?" Chase asked. "Seems risky, doesn't it?"

Stitts shrugged and turned to Detective Marsh.

"You have a map?"

Detective Marsh walked over to his desk and pulled open the top drawer. He pulled out a map and unfolded it about a dozen times before handing it to Stitts, who proceeded to tack it on the large board located off to one side.

"Seriously?" Chase mumbled. "Can't we just do this on the computer?"

Stitts frowned as he walked over to the desk and scooped up the case file. Without another word, he glanced at the page and then marked an X on the map. He repeated this three more times, and then drew a line connecting all four Xs in a diamond shape.

As Detective Marsh made his way over to the board, Stitts plunked the marker down in the center of the diamond shape.

"That's it," Marsh said, squinting heavily.

"What's *it*?" Chase asked.

"That spot. That's Club 101, the last place all three of these girls were seen alive. We're one step ahead of you."

Chapter 21

"THESE ARE ALL THE witness statements?" Chase asked, holding up several sheets of paper.

Detective Marsh nodded. He was smiling, clearly proud of putting a spear right in the middle of her theory. And while his claim that the last place all four girls had been seen was the club wasn't completely accurate — Leah and Bernice had been seen at Club 101 the night they died, while Kirsty and Meg were at the pub across the street — it was close enough.

It was possible that their killer had stalked his victims beforehand, given that witness statements confirmed that the girls liked to go out pretty much every weekend to the same locations. It was even possible that he stashed the tools somewhere around, or even inside the girls' apartments before being led back there.

And yet this didn't seem to jive with Chase. She couldn't shake the nagging sensation that something was very wrong with Detective Marsh's theory.

She had been inside Leah's head, and the girl hadn't been drugged when she was having sex with the unsub. In fact, she'd been happy, fulfilled. It wasn't out of the question that the man had sex with these girls first, and then something triggered him. Despite Stitts's claim that it was most likely their killer was someone who could never get the girl, this wasn't always the case. Bundy, Dahmer, and Manson had all been good-looking and charming. Manson could have any girl he wanted, and often did.

And yet… there was some sort of shadow clouding their judgment, something that didn't seem right, but that Chase couldn't quite place.

Chase pored over the pages of witness statements. Most were accounts from the victims' girlfriends, and none claimed that they had encountered anyone suspicious the night Bernice, Meg, Kirsty, and Leah were murdered. In fact, they all stated that their night had been relatively quiet with fewer potential suitors than they were used to. Anywhere between one and three a.m., they had parted ways and had taken a cab home or, in the victims' cases, walked.

Chase made a mental note of the similarity, that all of the victims lived within walking distance of the bar.

This reinforced Marsh's theory that the killer had stalked the victims beforehand, but also confirmed Chase's claim that their unsub didn't stand out in a crowd.

It was almost as if neither hers nor Marsh's theories were accurate, but neither could be completely discounted, either.

With a sigh, she tossed the pages on the desk and closed her eyes. She was so tired that she didn't even have the mental energy to prevent her mind from drifting.

Thankfully, she didn't think about Georgina, Brad, Felix, or even *brown sugar*; instead, she found herself remembering her time in Alaska. Chase thought about the bartender of The Barking Frog, about how he was charming and good-looking, how he had a way with women.

This is the type of person we're looking for, her mind implored.

And yet in that case, Brent Pine was only guilty of selling a teener of coke to some girls who were looking to party.

Ah, a hit would be awfully nice right now. Just a little—

"You got your undercover agents at the club?" Agent Stitts asked, startling her.

"Yeah," Marsh replied, looking up from his own stack of papers. "I have three men moving from the pub to the club and back as soon as they open — day and night. If they see anything out of the ordinary, they're going to move in."

Stitts chewed his lip.

"Make sure they're absolutely certain if they do," Stitts warned. "If our killer gets spooked, he might shut down, move elsewhere."

Detective Marsh grunted, as if to say, I'm no rookie, and then turned back to his papers.

The interruption gave Chase pause; their killer's prey was women with dark hair and pale features, and yet their undercovers were all men. It didn't seem to make sense to her.

She bit her tongue, and instead tried to focus on finding additional links between the victims. Something that might provide insight into their killer's motives.

Besides the obvious, that is.

"What about CCTV footage from inside the club or the pub?" Stitts asked.

Again, Detective Marsh nodded.

"Yeah, I'm having my guys head over to the club now to get footage from last night. We've already been through all the footage they had from when Bernice Wilson was last seen at the club, but we're giving it a second look. There were several guys who came up to her during the course of the night, but nothing out of the ordinary. We've also got our tech guys doing some state-of-the-art facial recognition on the people in the club that night, but most of the time it's too dark to run the software, or they aren't looking at the camera dead on. As for Meg and Kirsty, the pub only keeps footage for a few days when there's no incident, and the nights that they were killed had already been wiped."

Chase pictured Leah Morgan in her mind, the way she had been when she hugged and kissed the man at her doorstep before they entered.

"So, we have two murders taking place a month apart, both on a Saturday, then three weeks later on a Friday night. Then we have the most recent murder, Leah Morgan, in the middle of the week," Stitts said in a voice that implied he was mostly speaking to himself.

The man stood and made his way over to the board, upon which he had affixed the photographs of the victims along the perimeter of the map of Chicago.

"The weekend attacks make sense, given how busy these places would be. The middle of the week, however… how busy is this place, Club 101, on a Wednesday?"

The smile slid off Detective Marsh's face.

"I'm fifty-seven years old, twice divorced, with three kids in college. Does it look like I know how busy a club is on Wednesday?"

Agent Stitts nodded.

"Good point. I think I'm going to go have a chat with the proprietor of the club. Ask him some of these questions. Hopefully it's not busy on Wednesdays, and maybe they remember something."

Chase got the impression that Stitts was just getting fidgety and wanted to get out of the cramped office; Marsh had already told them that there was nothing on the tapes, and the man's statement that Chase had just finished reading revealed nothing of interest about the night in question.

Her eyes drifted to the board, and they fell on the image of Leah Morgan, her mouth open, a strip of duct tape hanging from one cheek.

"Any leads on the duct tape? The matchsticks?" Chase asked.

Detective Marsh reached for a folder on his desk that Chase hadn't gotten to yet and opened it. Then he started to read, or paraphrase, maybe.

"The duct tape is the most common brand in all of Chicago, can be bought at countless number of stores across the city. The matches have yet to be matched to anything local, but so far as we can tell, there's nothing special about them. Just Strike Anywheres."

Chase chewed the inside of her lip.

"What about fingerprints on the duct tape?"

"Nope. Nothing. No fingerprints on the matchsticks or the duct tape."

This struck Chase as odd.

"Couldn't pull any, or they were wiped?"

"Wiped."

"And what about the DNA from the semen found in the condoms?"

As if he knew this question was coming next, Detective Marsh had already flipped to a new page and started to read.

"Condoms were found in Leah, Bernice, and Meg's apartments. None was found in Kirsty's—the unsub probably flushed it. The sperm belongs to a male with no genetic diseases, likely Caucasian, unrelated to any of the victims. There were no matches in the system," he said as he snapped the folder closed. "Clearly, our guy knew he wasn't in the system and didn't care if he left DNA at the scene."

"Did you only check Chicago?" Stitts asked.

Detective Marsh nodded.

"Yeah, we only ran the DNA results through Chicago first, but I'll have my boys send it up to the feds—" Detective

Marsh offered a wry smile. "Shit, forgot, *you* guys are the feds."

"Tell your boys to send the results to Tony Acevedo at Quantico; cc me on the email, and we'll have the results from the nationwide database in a few days."

Chase was listening to what the men were saying to each other, but she wasn't really paying attention.

"Sounds good."

After a short pause, Stitts said, "Alright, I'm going to head out to the club to ask the proprietor a few questions about the foot traffic on a week night."

"Be my guest, but I doubt you'll find anything. And our men should be back soon with the footage from Wednesday night any minute."

"Have your guys run through it, see if there are any individuals that were there on both the night that Bernice was murdered and last night," Stitts said, before turning to Chase. "You coming?"

Why would a guy, who apparently had no problem picking up these women, sleep with them, and slit their throats afterward?

"Chase?"

And why did he tape their mouths? Put matchsticks to prop their eyes open? Why leave a condom and —

"You sure there were no fingerprints on the tape or matchsticks?" she asked quickly, raising her eyes.

Detective Marsh, who had been heading towards the door, whipped around to face her. He squinted, which caused the crow's feet at the corners of his eyes to lump together in one thick ravine. Clearly, he was trying to figure out if she was challenging him.

She wasn't—Chase just wanted to clarify the point.

"Positive. We checked them all and didn't pull so much as a partial."

"And that doesn't seem strange to you? The man leaves a condom full of his spunk in the wastebasket, but doesn't leave a single fingerprint on the tape?"

Chapter 22

"YOU FEEL THAT STRONGLY about this, huh?" Stitts asked from the driver's seat. "That the girls weren't coerced or dragged back to their homes?"

Chase had been right: Stitts wanted to get out of the precinct, and maybe away from Detective Marsh, for a little while.

And she didn't blame him; she too felt that while they had only been in Chicago for less than a day, things had quickly grown stale. It was a good idea to change locales in an attempt to spur some new ideas. And outside the location where the victims had been killed, the last of which Chase had already visited, what better place than the last location they were seen alive?

"Yeah, I do," Chase said softly. "When I touched Leah… when I touched her, I didn't get the impression that she was frightened in any way. She wasn't scared of the man she went home with, and while she was definitely drunk, I don't think she was high."

It felt good for Chase to verbalize how she felt, of not having to select her words carefully. Unlike with Detective Marsh, she didn't have to worry about saying something that might be construed as—what had Stitts called it? Voodoo?

Chase had no illusions of being a clairvoyant, didn't have time for such nonsense, and Stitts knew it too. Somewhere along the way, her mind had just figured out how to pick up on things that she wasn't consciously aware of, the order of the room for instance, the condom that she must have seen on the way in to the bedroom, but hadn't really noticed until the way out, the way the bed sheets were arranged, the location of the woman's purse. The fact that she was naked, but there weren't any clothes in or around the bed. Her mind had put together a narrative based on her subconscious observations, which had only come to the fore in the form of a strange, almost lucid dream when she'd touched Leah Morgan. She had no fucking idea how this happened, or why it just started back in Alaska, but after what had happened with Agent Martinez, she had learned to trust it.

And if there's one other person in this entire world who wouldn't doubt a gut instinct, it was FBI Special Agent Jeremy Stitts.

The man nodded as if he were following along with her thoughts.

"You mind if I play devil's advocate, then?" Stitts asked as he turned off the Kennedy Expressway. The precinct was only roughly fifteen minutes from Club 101, and they had already been driving for a good five before Stitts had started asking questions.

Ten minutes to break me down, Chase thought with a smirk. Her face hardened when her heart skipped a beat and her arm started to itch again.

"Go ahead."

"What if Detective Marsh is right? What if our killer is of low to average intelligence and doesn't know about DNA, but has seen enough cop shows to know about fingerprints? So, he wears gloves, but doesn't bother hiding his DNA. What if he just follows the girls home from the bar, jabs them in the neck with heroin, and then drags them inside to have his way with them?"

Chase stared at Stitts as he spoke. She had expected something more profound out of the man.

"Really? Well, for one, the injections were in the arm, not the neck. As for the DNA, the State of Illinois now requires you to give a DNA sample if you are just charged with a crime. So, if our unsub was convicted of a crime, and has his fingerprints on file, then he would also have his DNA taken too. And his lawyer, or the person taking the swab, would have explained it to him. I mean, there's a chance that he was arrested *before* they took DNA, or that he works for a government agency that takes fingerprints, but not DNA. Possible, but unlikely. The real questions we should be asking is why are all the girls recovered or recovering addicts? And why use a condom? Why is he worried about knocking these girls up, if he's going to kill them anyway?"

Stitts paused before answering.

"Maybe he was their drug dealer? Knows they're vulnerable? And maybe he uses a condom because the girls are… uh… unclean?"

Chase mulled this over for a moment. What had started out as her partner throwing simple challenges at her theory, had ended up in her questioning what she had 'seen.'

They just didn't have enough information; these weren't the typical murders, or murderer.

"I'll ask Marsh to check for venereal diseases when we get back," Stitts said at last.

They drove in silence for the next five or ten minutes, and Chase found herself drifting into her own head. This was not a good place to be, especially given that her arm had started to itch, and her skin had begun to crawl, reminding her that it had been more than a day since her last fix. And no matter how horrible that experience had been, there was always the *next* fix.

Another chance to forget.

Chase scratched furiously at her arm, but then caught Stitts looking at her out of the corner of his eye and stopped immediately.

She muttered something about fabric softener, and then something else about how Stitts should have let her bring some of her clothes with them to Chicago.

Stitts's eyes returned to the road and a few minutes later, he found a spot outside a bakery and parked the rental.

"Is just up there," Stitts said, pointing at a neon sign about two hundred meters from where they'd parked. Even in the midafternoon, the letters glowed so brightly that Chase could make them out from her vantage point in the passenger seat.

Club 101.

"All right, let's do this then."

Stitts reached for the door handle, but before opening it, he turned back to Chase one final time. There was concern in his eyes, concern that reminded Chase of when he had forced his way into her apartment and had found her with puke drying on her chin and chest.

"You going to be okay, Chase?"

Chase ground her teeth to fight the urge to scratch again, and opened her car door.

"I'll be fine," she lied as she stepped out. "I'll be fine."

Chapter 23

CHASE AND STITTS WALKED by Club 101 first, examining the street, imagining what it would be like on a busy Friday or Saturday night, as opposed to being nearly empty on a Thursday afternoon. Chase spotted the pub across the street, an Irish joint aptly named O'Cooper's Crown, not more than a block down. Her eyes skipped from the glitz and faux glamour of Club 101, to the purposeful dinginess of O'Cooper's.

Our killer has an eclectic range of drinking holes, she thought. *More concerned with finding his type of woman than he is with worrying about where he's going to be seen.*

"Should we go in?" Chase asked, suddenly feeling the need to get off the street. It had been warmer in Quantico than Chicago, but her eyes had apparently become sensitive to the sun at this latitude.

And it would be harder for Stitts to see her scratch at the millions of spiders that burrowed beneath her skin in the dank interior of the club than out here on the sidewalk.

"Not just yet," Stitts said absently.

With a scowl, Chase followed her partner past the club, trying to distract herself by taking in her surroundings, by imagining that she was the man that Leah had thrown her arms around.

There was a pizza joint next to the club, a shawarma place beside that. The third building housed some sort of gaming emporium the windows of which were covered in pictures of scantily clad women gripping broad-chested men who wielded comically large swords, clearly making up for comically small penises.

Across the street she spotted a Subway and a McDonald's, the latter of which actually showed some life.

Stitts seemed lost in his own head as he walked up and down the street, and Chase followed like a puppy dog, sneaking scratches at her arms whenever he peered into the windows of one of the shops or restaurants.

"You ready?" Stitts asked as they made their way back to Club 101.

Chase played it cool and shrugged. Even though the sun was shining above, she suddenly felt cold and clammy.

Fuck, ya, I'm ready. Ready to get out of the sun, she wanted to say.

"Ready when you are," she said with a forced smile.

Stitts reached for the door handle, but stopped short of pulling it, his eyes locked on hers.

"You okay?"

Chase frowned.

"Why do you keep asking me that?" she snapped.

Now it was Stitts's turn to shrug.

"You look tired, is all."

"Well, I am tired," Chase shot back. "And hungover. Still. Now can you please…"

Stitts's grip tightened on the handle and then he pulled the door wide.

At least that's what he tried to do. But the door was locked, and his hand slipped from the handle and he stumbled backward.

Chase smiled despite herself.

"How about we try this the old-fashioned way?" she said as she reached out and knocked on the blacked-out glass. It was only three-thirty in the afternoon, but she suspected that there would be someone inside. A stock boy perhaps, or bartender like Brent Pine, refilling the stocks for tonight.

Sure enough, in less than a minute, the door opened a crack.

"We're not open until eight," a phantom, nasally voice told them.

Without waiting for an answer, the door started to close, but Stitts, who had since recovered from his embarrassing stumble, reached out and succeeded in pulling it wide this time.

A short, squat man with beady black eyes and gray hair that started well beyond his forehead and fell to his shoulders, careened onto the sidewalk.

"Hey!" he shouted. Not wanting to make a scene, Stitts corralled the man and, in one smooth motion, all three of them stepped inside Club 101.

The man struggled in Stitts's grasp like a drunken penguin, but he was no contest for the FBI agent.

"Police! I'll call the police! Barney, get out here!"

Stitts let go of the man.

"Calm down," he said. The man's eyes went wide when Stitts reached into the inner pocket of his suit jacket—*oh, so he had time to pack his clothes,* Chase thought with a scowl—but then the man's expression flattened when Stitts pulled out his badge. "I'm FBI Agent Stitts, and this is my partner Agent Adams. We only want to ask you a few questions, is all. Didn't want to make a scene outside."

Chase was experiencing déjà vu: the interior of Club 101 was almost identical to The Barking Frog. This shouldn't have surprised her, given that most clubs had the same general layout and feel. Or so she'd heard. Club 101 came complete with all of the hallmarks characteristic of its namesake: dim lighting, the cloying odor of alcohol and sweat, a general paucity of seating. Things characteristic of a place designed for two things: to get people drunk and to get people laid.

The man in the suspenders shrugged and grumbled something about how a scene had already been made, before directing a comment at Stitts.

"I already told the *po*-lice everything I know—they just left after stealing our security footage. Those girls came in here, the ones that got themselves good and dead, but they was alive when they left. That's alls I know. I'm sick of the *po*-lice harassing me about it. Bad for business."

Chase felt anger build inside her as she pictured Leah's throat in tatters, the mattress upon which she lay so soaked with blood that it was spongy to the touch.

Got themselves good and dead.

Stitts likely sensed this as he stepped toward the man, in the process putting his body between gray hair and Chase.

"Just relax there, cowboy. We just have a few more questions, then we'll be out of your incredibly beautiful hair. And we're not the *po*-lice, by the way, we're the FBI."

Stitts finished by dramatically tapping the three letters prominently displayed on his badge, and Chase had to suppress a chuckle.

"I already told—"

A growl from the dark depths Drew both Stitts's and Chase's full attention.

A large figure brandishing some sort of weapon came sprinting at them, and Stitts instinctively shoved the short man out of the way.

Then both he and Chase drew their service pistols.

"Stop!" Chase shouted, her hands trembling. "Stop or I'll put a bullet in your brain!"

Chapter 24

THE MAN IMMEDIATELY DROPPED the weapon, which Chase saw was some sort of archaic baseball bat, and it clattered to the floor.

"Barney! Relax, it's the feds," the proprietor said as he collected himself.

The large man, whose name was apparently Barney, held up his hands and took two giant steps backwards. Stitts slid his gun back into his holster, and then gently put pressure on the top of Chase's arm until she lowered hers. Her hands were trembling so badly that it took her three tries to put the gun in her holster.

"A little jumpy around here, aren't we?" Stitts said to no one in particular.

"Yeah, well, in case you haven't heard, there's been some murders around here lately," the squat man replied.

Chase shot the man a look.

Her heart was thrumming in her chest, not because of the danger that Barney had posed—in reality, both she and Stitts had overreacted; the man had been a good fifteen or twenty feet away with only a bat as his weapon—but because of her finger. Chase's finger had been twitching something fierce and she could only guess what might've happened had it slipped on the trigger.

Get a grip, Chase. Get a fucking grip before you do something that you can't undo, something that even Stitts can't bail you out of.

"This your head of security?" Stitts asked.

The squat man nodded.

"Yeah, that's Barney, Barney Redman. He's my friend's son. Looks after things around here when I can't."

Can't came out sounding like *cain't*.

Chase racked her brain and finally came up with the man's name from the witness statements that Detective Marsh had provided her.

"And you must be Bruce Ibsen," she said.

The man nodded.

"Always have been, always will be, I suspect."

Stitts, clearly annoyed, shook his head and pressed his lips together tightly.

"All right, enough of this. I just want to ask you a few questions, then we'll be out of here."

Evidently, seeing their pistols up close had changed Bruce Ibsen's opinion on whether or not he should answer their questions.

"Fine. Barney, you go back to keep stocking the shelves."

"No, he should stay," Chase said. "I have a few questions for him to."

Neither man nodded, but neither moved either.

"So, we know that the two girls were here—Leah Morgan and Bernice Wilson—and we know that Bernice was here on a Saturday, while Leah attended your classy establishment just two nights ago," Stitts began. As he spoke, Chase eyed Barney and Bruce carefully. Bruce was fidgeting, but she suspected based on his appearance and the way he'd reacted when they pulled their guns, that the man fidgeted all the time. Barney, on the other hand, who stood at least six feet four, had a dumb expression plastered on his face and didn't move at all. His hands were still in the air, palms toward them. "So why don't we start easy… how many people do you usually have here on a Saturday night?"

A creepy smile broke out on Bruce's face.

"We're the busiest joint in town. Well, maybe not in town," he admitted, "but at least in the Northeast."

Stitts's eyes narrowed.

"How many people, Bruce, not how many Instagram followers you have."

Chase raised an eyebrow, surprised at the Instagram reference. Stitts couldn't have been more than a few years older than her, mid-thirties at the latest, but he didn't strike her as a man who spent too much of his time online.

And I bet I don't strike him as a woman with an awful heroin habit, either, she scolded herself. *The faces people show aren't always their real faces. Don't forget about Brent Pine, Ryanne Elliot, Chris Martinez. Dr. Mark Kruk.*

Bruce Ibsen poked his tongue into his cheek and looked up and to the left as he thought about the question.

"Well, we get about, uhhh, I'm to say three-hundred fifty, maybe four hundred, four-hundred fifty on a really good weekend."

Stitts nodded.

"And on a Wednesday?"

Bruce Ibsen shrugged.

"Now that I can't tell ya; I don't work on Wednesdays, only on the weekend."

Stitts turned to Barney Redman next.

"You can put your hands down," he said.

The man did as he was ordered. Chase continued to watch him carefully and marveled at the fact that since they had entered Club 101, she hadn't seen Barney blink. Not once.

"You work on Wednesdays?" Chase asked.

The big man nodded.

"Yes, ma'am. I work every day," he said slowly.

Ma'am? What is with this ma'am shit? Do I really look that old these days?

"And last Wednesday, how many people would you say you had in here? Just a rough estimate?"

The man raised a bushy eyebrow.

"You mean like last Wednesday? Or like two days ago?"

Chase shook her head, trying not to let her annoyance overwhelm her.

"I mean two days ago when the girl was murdered."

Barney nodded again.

"Oh, I can't be sure, but I'm thinking maybe twenty? Or maybe not. Could be fifty. I'm not too good with numbers."

Chase stared for a moment, and then shifted her eyes to look at Stitts whose expression matched hers.

Okay, so anywhere between twenty and fifty.

It was clear that as much as it pained her to admit it, Detective Marsh was right. They were just wasting their time here.

"Okay, you guys have been a great help. Spectacular help," Stitts said. "Just be careful with that baseball bat, wouldn't want you striking anybody by accident."

"Thank you, and I will be careful," Barney Redman said in his flat affect.

Chase, still a little bewildered as to what had just happened, followed Stitts out into the sun.

When the door was firmly closed behind them, she turned to her partner.

"Well, you're looking for somebody of below average to average intelligence," she said with a hint of a smile. "You think maybe Barney Redman's our guy? You think that he charmed those girls with his excellent command of the English language?"

Now it was Stitts's turn to hold his hands up defensively.

"All right, you win."

Chase's stomach suddenly grumbled, and although she hadn't thought about using for the last few minutes, she'd thought about eating.

"What do I win? A meal?"

Stitts looked around.

"In this gastronomic utopia? Sure thing—it's on me."

Chapter 25

CHASE WIPED GARLIC MAYO from the corner of her mouth and then swallowed a piece of slow-cooked beef. Stitts stared at her as she ate, a disgusted look on his face.

"Really? You like this stuff? How the hell do you stay so thin?"

Chase shrugged.

The truth was, she didn't really like it *that* much, but of the options on the street, she had deemed it the most likely to fill her up, fill the void.

"It's not bad. And I stay thin by running through the woods with a bullet in my side, trying to get away from a demented madman who thinks I had something to do with his sister's death."

Chase had meant it as a joke, but when the words came out of her mouth, it suddenly didn't feel that funny.

Stitts stared at her like a beached walleye for several moments before turning his attention to his potatoes. The fried spuds were buried beneath a heaping glob of the garlic/mayo combo, despite having asked for the man behind the sneeze guard to go light on the sauce. He used his plastic fork to pick through the mound as if rooting for gold among the russets, before finding one that suited his fancy. He plopped it unceremoniously into his mouth, chewed it twice, and then grimaced dramatically as he swallowed.

"Oh, fuck off," Chase said with a laugh. She had observed the entire charade with abject fascination. "It's not that bad. And when you just need something to fill—wait a second. Wait a second."

Stitts grew serious again.

"What? What is it?"

"These girls... these girls went to either the pub or the club, right?"

Stitts nodded.

"Yeah."

"Well, what do people do after they've indulged in one too many?"

Stitts picked up a potato with a quivering dollop of mayonnaise on top.

"They get something to eat."

"That's right."

Chase looked around, trying to locate a CCTV camera inside the shawarma joint. She didn't see any, but that didn't necessarily mean there wasn't one hidden somewhere.

"We should get Detective Marsh and his men out here, get them to check out all the food places to see if there's any video of our girls eating after the bar."

Stitts nodded and took the phone out of his pocket and started to dial, twirling the skewered potato in his other hand as he did.

As Stitts waited for the detective to answer, Chase leaned forward.

"Didn't your mother ever tell you not to play with your food? Give that to me."

***

"Stomach contents," Chase said. "We should see what the girls ate last."

Detective Marsh squinted at her from across the desk.

"And you want to do this... why? You think that our perp targeted them while they were wolfing down after-bar grub as opposed to inside the club?"

No shit, Sherlock, Chase almost blurted. She managed to bite her tongue at the last second.

"You got it," Stitts answered for her.

"My foot soldiers tell me that only the McDonald's has a CCTV feed. They're going over the footage now."

Stitts simply stared, implementing a technique that Chase was only just starting to get used to. Instead of asking the question again and risk unnerving the other party, the man would just stare, silently coercing the person into answering without being queried a second time.

It appeared to Chase that, with time, Marsh would come around.

But she lacked the man's resolve. And, besides, she was feeling especially irritable today.

"What about the stomach contents?" she asked.

Marsh presented a sour expression before answering.

"Yeah, all right. I'll give a call in the morgue and see what they can do. "

Chase nodded her approval. She was beginning to think that she was on to something, that maybe the thing that all four women had in common wasn't so much where they had started the night, but where they had finished it.

Chase checked her watch and saw that it was coming on five in the afternoon.

"What about tonight? You going to have men stationed in the club when it opens?"

Detective Marsh nodded.

"Yeah, every night here on out. I'm going to give a briefing at around seven—you are more than welcome to attend."

Chase shrugged.

"I'll go."

"Me too," Stitts added. "It'll be good to introduce ourselves. Hopefully we won't be here long—hopefully we catch this bastard before he strikes again—but I just want to let your men know that we're here to lend a hand wherever we can. Which leaves us just enough time to—"

Chase shook her head.

"No, you misunderstood. I'll go to the club, undercover."

Agents Stitts, who had been standing at the board, turned to look at her, a stern expression etched on his face.

"Chase, I don't think that's a good idea."

"No, it makes sense. This guy's out hunting women, and I look enough like them. My hair's maybe not long enough, and maybe it's a lighter brown than the victims, but in the dark club it'll be hard to tell. Maybe we get lucky and he picks me out of the crowd."

Stitts took another step towards her, shaking his head the entire time.

"This is your first case, Chase," he said softly. "And after what happened with Martinez, I don't think that—"

"You know what? That *is* a good idea," Detective Marsh interrupted, chewing on the end of his pen. "I don't have any female detectives on staff, and while I'm sure I can dig up someone from another precinct, that'll take time. And then we got to get lucky to find someone who fits the profile."

Stitts didn't seem to hear Detective Marsh as he made his way over to her.

"Chase, I really—"

"I can do it," Chase said without hesitation. "Stitts, it's our best shot."

An awkward silence ensued during which Stitts continued to stare at Chase, while Detective Marsh made no effort to hide his curiosity.

Why is he trying to protect me? Chase wondered. *He couldn't possibly know… could he?*

Chase decided that even though Stitts was technically her superior, she would get enough backing from Marsh to go through with this.

She closed the folder and stood.

"I'm doing this, Stitts. Whether you want me to or not."

Stitts's face contorted, and she knew in that moment that the man had accepted defeat.

"Can we just go for a ride first?"

"Where to?" she asked hesitantly.

"The rehab clinic. See if we can dig something up on our victims."

Chase grimaced. The last thing she wanted to do right now was be in the presence of people who were addicted to heroin.

People like herself.

"Chase? Please."

Chapter 26

"YOU DON'T NEED TO protect me, you know," Chase said as she flopped into the passenger seat. "I'm not a child."

Stitts employed his will of silence then, and even though Chase knew what the man was doing, she was helpless to keep quiet.

"I'm fine—I'll be fine. Jesus."

Stitts still said nothing, and Chase sulked.

She watched the city go by through the filter of the tinted window, seeing, but not really acknowledging, the shrinking buildings, the gradual thinning of cars around them. The general paucity of street lights.

After ten minutes, Chase's surroundings became nondescript, no longer belonging to the sprawling metropolis that was Chicago, but a homage to perhaps every small town in America.

Like Franklin, Tennessee, where Chase had been born and raised. As they drove on, Stitts passed something that she never thought she would see less than twenty miles from the center of Chicago: a farm. Chase spotted a cow grazing on the brown grass, and in the distance, she saw a handful of sheep, their coats still damp and thin from the recently passed winter. The sheep reminded Chase of the Williamson County Fair that she and her family used to attend every year. The Fair that she and Georgina had been walking home from that day…

***

"Stay with your father, girls. I'm going to talk to the Mayor for a few minutes," Kerry Adams said.

Chase nodded, looking around for her dad. She spotted him standing in front of one of the carnival games, the same one that she had wasted all of her allowance on trying to beat, but hadn't won once, not even a consolation prize. Keith Adams was standing next to the thin man in the straw hat who ran the rigged game, a red plastic cup clutched in his meaty palm.

Cool fingers suddenly squeezed her cheeks and turned her head.

"Don't go wandering off, now. Stay close," Kerry ordered, her expression stern. Her mother's breath smelled mildly of gin, which wasn't altogether off-putting given the general smell of animal feces that clung to the humid air.

"Yes, Mom," Chase whispered, casting her eyes downward. The fingers clenched, and she looked up again.

"And keep an eye on your sister, would you? I'm counting on you, Chase."

Chase nodded, and her mother continued to hold her face for a good three seconds before finally letting go.

Even though the icy grip was gone, Chase could still feel where the tight digits had squeezed her cheeks.

"Good," Kerry said, a smile returning to her pretty face. The woman smoothed the front of her white dress and then stood to full height.

She was taller than most women, with long, tanned legs the color of melted toffee. Chase hoped to look like her mother one day, based on how she saw others turn and stare whenever she walked by.

And Chase was tall for her age, although lately her classmates had started to catch up to her.

"You have any allowance left?" Kerry asked.

Chase looked back to where her father was standing and still talking with the man in the straw hat.

"No," she admitted, almost ashamed.

"What about you, Georgie?"

When there was no immediate answer, Chase looked down at her younger sister. Predictably, the girl was standing with her eyes locked on the teacups that went whipping around a central axis at breakneck speeds. Even though Chase didn't even focus on the ride, just catching them turning in her periphery made her stomach lurch.

The idea of riding the thing was enough to make her feel nauseous.

"Georgie?"

The girl turned around and offered a wide smile and then she bounded over to Chase.

"I want to go on the cups," she said with a lisp. "The fast cups."

Chase shook her head.

"No way, I'll puke."

"C'mon, I'll go by myself. You just watch. It looks fun!"

Chase shook her head again, swallowing hard.

"Here, Chase, take your sister on the ride," her mother said, pressing a five-dollar bill into her palm. "Just remember, keep an eye on your sister. You know how she gets around shiny things."

Shiny things...

Chase giggled.

"Okay, Mom."

Kerry cast one final, furtive glance over at her husband, before adding, "And stay close to your dad, okay?"

Chase said she would for what felt like the hundredth time, and with another smile, this one somewhat sad, her mother turned and made her way behind the carnival rides.

Chase watched as she passed a sign that read 'Employees Only,' and despite the fact that her mom most definitely wasn't an employee, Chase knew no one would say anything.

It was her long, tanned legs. Even at her age, even at the ripe age of seven, Chase knew that legs like those would take you anywhere.

She blinked, and her mother was gone.

"Georgie, there's no way I'm going on the teacups. I'll puke for sure. I—Georgie?" Chase whipped around, her eyes scanning the yellow grass, the colorful booths, the carnival games.

The noise from competing games and rides was suddenly overwhelming, and instead of shrieks of joy, all Chase heard were screams of agony.

Her dad was still there by the stupid, impossible game where you had to throw a softball into a basket that was hanging on its side, his mouth open in laughter.

But Georgie... she couldn't see her sister anywhere.

"Georgie!" Chase cried. "Georgie, where are you?"

Panic started to grip her, and she felt her heart begin to gallop in her chest. The heat ensured that she had been sweating from the moment she had awoken, but now her body suddenly felt as if it was soaked, like she had just jumped out of a pool.

"Georgie! Georgie! Geor—"

A hand brushed up against her hip and she spun around.

"Oh, thank goodness!" Chase cried. After relief slowed her racing heart, she scowled down at her sister's freckled face. "Where'd you go? Where'd you go?"

Georgina shrugged and fluttered her eyelids.

"I told you I wanted to go on the cups," she whined.

Chase reached out and grabbed her sister's shoulder a little harder than she'd intended.

"Ow," Georgie cried, but Chase ignored her.

"Just stay close to me, okay? Don't run off."

Georgina nodded, and Chase let go of her shoulder. Staring at the crumpled bill in her hand, Chase said, "There's no way I'm going on that ride, but I could sure go for something cold? A snocone, maybe? What do you think?"

Chapter 27

"**WAKE UP, CHASE—YOU'RE** shaking."

Chase's eyes snapped open. Her body was covered in a cold sweat, and her vision was blurred.

What the hell happened… one minute I'm looking out the window, the next I'm back at the Williamson County Fair. I must have fallen asleep, I must—

"You've got a habit of doing that, don't you?" Stitts said as he pulled into the parking lot outside a nondescript brown brick building.

Chase cleared her throat and sat up in her seat.

"Doing what?" she croaked, wiping the sweat from her brow. She blinked rapidly, and eventually her vision cleared.

"Falling asleep in my car."

"Sorry," she offered. "Just tired, is all."

Stitts didn't answer, and Chase got the impression that her excuses were wearing thin with the man. There was a time when she had been confident in her ability to read his tells, but either Stitts had become more guarded recently, or she was more distracted.

She had no idea what he was thinking and staring for any longer would only serve to make things more awkward.

Chase adjusted her sunglasses and then opened the car door. In the process, she caught part of her reflection in the side mirror. There were several red marks on her neck, and she instinctively rubbed at them, remembering the creep who had grabbed her back in Woodbridge.

And how she had slapped him in the face with a urine-soaked tampon. The memory almost made her laugh.

Almost.

Straightening her back, she stared at the brick building before them. There were silver letters over the large doors that read, "Palisades," but there was no indication that this was an addiction treatment center.

"Well," she asked, now scratching absently at her arm. "What's the plan here, boss? This is your gig, remember."

Stitts strode toward the building and Chase followed.

"The plan is to figure out if Leah and Kirsty went here with the other girls. I'm hoping to grab a staff and patient list, figure out if it's all just a coincidence."

The man sighed, and Chase looked over at her partner.

For the first time since the day that she'd found him bound and bloodied at the foot of his bed, he looked tired to her.

Exhausted, even.

"We're here to find a killer, Chase," he said, without looking at her. "Don't forget that."

Forget that? How the hell can I forget that?

***

"But it's right there, isn't it?" Stitts asked with a sly grin. He aimed his chin at the stack of folders on the lower level of the desk.

The woman, a pleasant looking lady with short blond hair tucked behind her ears and bright green eyes, offered a tired smile.

"I would really like to help," she said softly. "But the best I can do is give you the list of employees. I'm afraid I can't tell you who my patients are. What we do here… well, it's *sensitive*, of course."

Chase looked the woman up and down. While she appeared compassionate to their cause—clearly, she had known Bernice and Meg—it was also clear that she was unfailing in her resolve. What she did here was indeed *sensitive*, and the Associate Director of Palisades Recovery would do her best to keep it that way.

Stitts, however, didn't appear to notice this and continued to press.

"Look, I get it, and I don't want to push. But there's no patient confidentiality after death. And that's, unfortunately, what has happened, and what we're trying to prevent from happening again. We know that Bernice Wilson and Meg Docker were treated here, their parents and friends told us; we just want to know if Leah Morgan and Kirsty Buchanan were also here. Most of all, though, we just want to catch the bastard who did this and stop him before he does it again."

The woman, who had introduced herself as Susan Datcher, sighed heavily, her ample bosom swelling beneath an aging cotton sweater.

"I know. Trust me, I know. And I want nothing more than to help."

Chase nodded.

"But you can't. I get it."

Stitts shot her a look, and Chase deliberately glanced to the folder on the desk before nodding at Susan.

It took a moment before Stitts caught on.

And then he shook his head.

"Well, thank you, Susan. Can we have a copy of your employee list, then? And a card, if you have it."

The woman nodded and reached over the side of the desk. Chase hoped that Susan would have to go to the cabinet by the back wall, or better yet to another room to get the file, but she had no such luck.

Susan opened a folder directly beside the one that Chase was suddenly certain contained a list of past and present patients.

After glancing briefly at the sheet of paper, Susan handed it to Stitts.

"Here's a list of all present employees," she took a business card from the holder on the desk and held out a card to him. "If you want a list of past employees, I'll have to dig them up. Just give me a call and I'll do that for you. Like I said, I really do want to help."

Stitts nodded.

"Thanks," he said, tapping the sheet of paper against an open palm. "And if I wanted to talk to one of your employees? How might I go about that?"

"That won't be a problem, but I would request that you come to me first so that I can bring them to you. We have several private conference rooms you can use, if you want."

Clearly, the woman was smart as well as shrewd; she didn't want them sneaking into the building under the guise of speaking to an employee just so that they could peek into one of the rooms.

That wasn't their goal, of course—the people they were interested in were already dead—but the woman was clearly thinking ahead.

"Thanks again, Susan. And we—"

Movement down the hallway caught Chase's attention and she leaned to look around Susan's frame. A man in a dark black button-down shirt emerged from one of the rooms and looked up. Their eyes met, and the blood instantly drained from his face.

"Who's that?" Chase interrupted.

Susan glanced over her shoulder.

"That's Craig—he's there, on the employee list. He's—"

"—gonna run!" Chase shouted.

Stitts's chin dissolved into his neck.

"He what?"

Chase wagged a finger in the man's direction.

"He's going to *run*!"

Stitts turned, and in that moment, the man did exactly as Chase said he would: he turned and started to sprint down the hallway.

"Shit!" Stitts cried as he shoved by Susan and started after him.

Chapter 28

"**CRAIG? CRAIG!** *STOP!*" **SUSAN** shouted as Stitts took after the man in the black shirt.

Chase's first instinct was to run after Stitts, but with Susan's back turned…

Without thinking, she reached over the counter and snatched the folder. Then she pulled off a minor miracle by untucking the back of her blouse and shoving it into her pants in one motion. Only then did she run after Stitts.

Craig turned the corner so quickly that his sneakers skidded across the tiled floor and his shoulder slammed against the wall. Stitts was gaining on him, and only a few seconds after they disappeared out of sight, Chase heard a grunt and then what sounded like a sack of wet potatoes falling to the ground.

Chase herself cleared the corner so quickly that she was barely able to stop before falling on top of her partner and the man Susan had called Craig.

The two of them were splayed out on the floor, with Stitts on top. His elbow and forearm were pressing hard against the base of the man's skull, pushing his face into the tiles. Craig's face was red, and he was breathing in wet hisses.

Stitts grunted as he reached behind him and pulled a set of cuffs from the back of his belt. As he did, the man started to struggle, and Stitts was nearly thrown off him as he tried to twist Craig's arms behind his back. Chase drove her heel onto the ball of the man's ankle and he cried out. Distracted by the pain, Stitts managed to cuff him.

"Get up," Stitts instructed, trying to hoist the man to his feet. His first attempt failed, however, as Chase was still grinding her heel into his ankle. Her partner looked over at her, nodded at her foot, and Chase reluctantly pulled it back.

"Alright, big boy, you wanna tell me why you ran?" Stitts asked once they were both standing.

The man grunted and clenched his jaw.

"Why'd you run?" Chase demanded, stepping in front of Craig. Her heart was thudding away in her chest, and it wasn't just because of the short jog down the hallway. "Did you run because you murdered those girls? Slit their throats? Let me ask you something, Craig, did you rape Meg and Bernice with the beer bottle before or after they were dead?"

Stitts gave her a strange look, but Chase ignored it. She reached forward and grabbed the collar of the man's shirt and pulled hard.

"Is that why, you sick fuck?"

"Chase," Stitts said, trying to stem the dam.

Craig's eyes widened, but only for a moment; they quickly transitioned into slits.

"I don't know what you're talking about, psycho."

"The fuck you don't," Chase spat, pulling even harder on the man's collar. Their faces were but an inch apart now. "How would you like it if I shoved a beer bottle up your—"

"Chase," Stitts snapped, his eyes darting over her shoulder.

Chase turned to see Susan Datcher approaching, her eyes wide, her mouth twisted in a frown. She let go of Craig's shirt and shoved him backward hard enough that Stitts had to plant his feet to avoid both of them toppling.

"Why'd you run, Craig?" Stitts repeated in a stern tone.

The man said nothing, but his body went limp when he saw Susan approach.

"Why, Craig?" Susan asked calmly.

Craig lowered his gaze, and for a moment it looked like he was going to stay quiet, that they were going to have to drag him back to the station to see if Detective Marsh could pry anything out of him.

But Chase was getting the distinct impression that Susan Datcher was more than just the Associate Director of Palisades Recovery; despite the small sample size, Chase thought that Susan was like a mother to these people.

To the addicts.

"Check my pocket," Craig said with a sigh.

Stitts reached into the man's pocket and pulled out a Ziploc bag full of white pills.

"Craig!" Susan gasped.

"I'm sorry," the man grumbled, not raising his eyes. "I just… I was…"

Chase reached out and snatched the bag from Stitts's hand. She held it up to the light and pushed the pills around until she could read the markings on one of them.

"Fifty-four, one-hundred forty-two," she said.

Susan's frown deepened.

"Methadone? Why the hell do you have methadone?"

Chase lowered the pills and stared at Craig. Her initial instinct when Craig had bolted was that he was their man, but now, staring at his pale features, the way he fidgeted, the fact that he was a wire rack beneath his clothes, she wasn't so sure.

The only thing 'Craig' looked like to her now was an addict. A sad, pathetic addict.

"I'm sorry," the man grumbled. "I was just…"

"Just what?" Chase snapped. Addict or not, she had to be sure about this.

Craig raised his eyes, which blazed into her.

"Fine. I was selling the damn stuff, okay? You happy now? I was trying to make a buck by selling the pills."

The man's eyes shifted upward and to the right as he spoke.

"Craig, c'mon," Susan offered in a condescending tone. "What were you thinking? Why would—"

"He's lying," Chase said.

Susan and Stitts both turned to look at her.

"I'm not, I'm selling the pills, I told you. I'm—"

Chase nonchalantly tucked the bag into the pocket of her jeans.

"It's bullshit. What sort of addict would use methadone to get high? How many pills would you even have to take, Craig? Five? Ten? That's if you didn't die first."

Craig struggled in Stitts's grasp, and her partner pushed the man's palms further up his back to control him.

"I... I dunno, I just sell—"

Chase shook her head.

"He's not selling the pills, Susan. He's using them to cut with the real shit—with heroin."

Craig pressed his lips together, but when he didn't immediately deny the claim, Chase knew it to be true.

"Goddammit, Craig; after all the work we've put in? After all this time," Susan said.

Chase stopped this runaway pity train before the coal engine fired up.

"Where were you Wednesday night, huh? Did you go down to the bar scene, pray on a recovering addict? Get your—"

"He was here," Susan interjected.

"What?" Chase spat.

"Craig… he was here at Palisades all night on Wednesday."

Chase blinked. Unlike when Craig had said he was selling the pills, Susan appeared to be telling the truth.

And why wouldn't she be? Why would she lie? Unless, of course, she had something to do with…

Chase shook her head.

"You sure?"

Susan nodded.

"Craig helps serve snacks during our meetings, and if he's feeling particularly…" Susan paused, clearly searching for the right word. Even in this situation, with Craig handcuffed and caught with a bag full of stolen methadone pills, she refused to call him for what he really was: an addict. "He was here Wednesday night. I'm positive."

Chase's eyes flicked back and forth.

Stitts acted first, yanking Craig's arms upward before unlocking them.

"What are you doing? You just going to let him go?" Chase snapped.

Stitts shrugged.

"What are we going to do? Arrest him for stealing methadone? You heard Susan, he was here Wednesday night."

Susan nodded, and her demeanor, which Chase had considered pleasant when they had first arrived, suddenly started to annoy her.

Mother hen protecting her flock. What if Craig wasn't *here and Susan's only covering for him?*

"So *she* says," Chase barked.

"Chase, please," Stitts said, finally letting go of Craig.

The man raised his eyes to look at Chase then, and goddammit if the man wasn't smirking at her. She raised her hand and stepped forward.

"You little fu—"

Stitts grabbed her arm and gently lowered it to her side.

"Cool it," he whispered in her ear. Then, to Susan, he said, "I've got your card. If there's anything else, I'll give you a call. Thanks for your help."

Susan smiled and nodded.

"I'm just sorry I couldn't be of *more* help. And don't worry about Craig, I'll take care of him."

Chase frowned.

"I'm sure you will," she said. Stitts put a hand on the small of her back and guided her down the hallway and toward the entrance.

"Thanks again, Susan."

"And the pills?" the woman asked, her eyebrows raising. "They're quite expensive, and as you can see, funding is tight."

Chase reluctantly reached into her pocket and pulled out the bag. Then she tossed it at the woman and turned away from her without seeing if she managed to catch it.

When they eventually made it back to Stitts's car, night had begun to descend on Chicago and a chill had started to embrace the air.

"Well that was a colossal waste of time," Stitts said with a sigh when they were both tucked safely inside the vehicle.

Chase reached behind her and pulled the folder out of her pants.

"Not completely," she said, tossing it onto Stitts's lap.

Stitts simply stared at the folder for a moment, resisting the urge to touch it.

"Is this...?"

Chase nodded and then curled onto her side. As she did, she slipped a finger into her jean pocket and scooped out one of the methadone pills she had taken from the Ziploc bag.

"As Drake says, you can thank me later," Chase whispered, before tucking the pill under her tongue. "Wake me when we get there. I need to rest up if I'm to be clubbing all night."

Chapter 29

"But I really want to go on the teacups!" Georgie whined. *"Like, really, really wanna go!"*

Chase sighed and wiped sweat from her forehead with the back of her hand. It was coming on three in the afternoon, and it was pretty much the hottest day in the history of the world.

She loved going to the Fair—loved the lights, the sounds, the smells—but today… today she had woken up with a headache and a nagging sensation that it wasn't going to be a good day. Her mother had made her favorite, banana pancakes, but she had had only a few bites before she felt uncomfortably full.

Getting dressed, she'd gotten her bracelet caught on her favorite shirt, a pale pink T with a cloud across the chest, which was emblazoned in rhinestones that formed the words 'Dream Big,' and had torn a good three-inch gash in the side.

That, in and of itself, wasn't so bad, but when her mother had seen the small rip, she'd insisted that Chase change her shirt.

Chase didn't want to change her shirt; she loved her Dream Big T-shirt.

"Everyone will be there, Chase," her mother had hissed. "Everyone will be watching. Just go change your shirt."

Chase swallowed audibly as she watched the teacups whip around.

"No," she said quietly. She didn't want to let her sister down, but there was literally no way in hell she was going on the vomit-inducer. Not today, anyway. "Please, Georgie. Ask Dad and maybe he can take you tomorrow. I just can't do it."

Georgie stared up at her, tears in her wide blue eyes.

"But—"

Chase looked away.

"No, I can't. Let's just go get a snow cone, okay? Please."

Georgie's lower lip curled, and her shoulders slumped in a sulk, but she eventually nodded.

"Fine. Whatever."

Chase felt her spirits perk somewhat now that she'd convinced Georgie that the teacups were out of the question. Even though she was two, almost three years older than her sister, it was clear who held the power in the relationship. After all, Georgie was the cute one, the special one, the one with the bright red hair and striking blue eyes, the one who people in the grocery store would always stop for and comment, remark that her hair was so beautiful. That she was so beautiful. Chase wasn't entirely bitter about this, however; if anything, it was a relief not to be the center of attention all the time. But sometimes, when Georgie got her way...

They walked hand-in-hand toward the snow cone vendor, a small, pop-up trailer, trying not to shuffle their feet in the dead grass and kick up any loose dirt and dried horse poop.

They waited in the short line in silence, still holding hands. When the group in front of them finally cleared, they stepped forward.

A man sporting an apron so stained with rainbow-colored snow cone syrup that it looked like a unicorn had used it as toilet paper, leaned out the window. He had the hairiest arms that Chase had ever seen, and each of these thick, black hairs glistened with sweat.

"What can I get you, ladies?" the man asked in a southern drawl. His cheeks were sunken, and when he smiled, Chase saw that he was missing one of his front teeth. She had never seen the man before; Chase and her family had been attending the Williamson County Fair for as long as she could remember. And during that time, only one man ran the snow cone pop-up: Mr. Robin-Graff. He was the same man who owned the car repair shop in Franklin, the one that her mother frequented almost every week it seemed.

"Blueberry, peeeas," Georgie said with a grin.

"Sure thing, shug," the man said, before turning to Chase. "What about you? You got a flavor in mind?"

Chase opened her mouth to ask for her favorite—watermelon—but then closed it.

"Where's Mr. Robin-Graff?" she asked instead.

The man's eyes flicked to the right, and for a split second his smile faltered.

"He's got the flu," the man said, his smile returning with more fervor.

You're lying, Chase thought.

But before she could call him on the lie—and she very well might have—Georgie tugged on her arm.

"Hurry up, Chase! I'm thuuursty!"

"Okay, okay," Chase said, looking up at the smiling, one-toothed man who most definitely was not Mr. Robin-Graff. "Watermelon."

The man nodded.

"Sure thing, ladies. One blueberry and one watermelon snow cone comin' right up."

The man receded into the trailer and, as he did, Chase stepped onto her tippy-toes and peered inside.

The shaved ice maker and the large tubs of fluorescent syrup were off to the right, but that wasn't what caught her eye.

To the left, behind the man who was preparing their snow cones, was something that immediately drew her attention.

Mr. Robin-Graff was famous in Franklin and the surrounding counties not just because of his snow cones and his auto repair shop, but also because he was notorious for wearing a red flannel shirt, no matter the temperature.

Chase recalled just a few weeks ago when her mom had left her and her sister in the waiting room while she'd gone to visit Mr. Robin-Graff who was working in the garage at the time. It was nearly as hot then as it was now, and the man was still wearing the flannel shirt. It had been a bit darker because of his sweat, and there had been grease on the breast pockets, but he was still wearing it.

And that was what she saw now: Mr. Robin-Graff's red flannel shirt. It was lying on the floor, and Chase could see that one of the sleeves had been entirely ripped off.

"Here you go, girls," the man said, returning to the window. He held a blue snow cone in one hand and a red one in the other. "Blueberry and watermelon, just as you ordered."

Chase, her brow still furrowed in confusion, took both and then handed the blue one to her sister.

She reached into her pocket and pulled out the crumpled five-dollar bill that her mother had given her.

"Here," she said, holding it out to the man.

Instead of taking it, he leaned out the window, crossing both hairy arms over the opening.

"It's on the house, young lady," he said with a smile.

For some reason, despite the heat, Chase suddenly felt a chill.

"Where's Mr. Robin-Graff?" she asked again.

The man stopped smiling.

"I told you, he's sick."

"Why is his shirt on the floor?"

The man didn't turn to look.

"Why don't you get out of here, kid? Get lost. Scram."

Chase stepped away from the window.

"Why don't you tell me what happened to Mr. Robin-Graff?"

The man's eyes narrowed to slits.

"Why don't you —"

Chase instinctively reached for her sister, to guide her protectively behind, but her hand only swatted warm humid air.

She whipped around.

Georgina wasn't just gone from her side, but Chase couldn't see her anywhere.

"Georgie!"

Panic began to set in as Chase searched the crowd for her sister's mop of red hair.

"Georgie! Georgie!"

Chapter 30

THE METHADONE TAB DIDN'T get Chase high, but it definitely took the edge off. She was grateful, given that she now found herself on display, and while she normally wasn't shy in front of a crowd, given her recent issues, she suddenly felt uncomfortable.

And hot; it felt like it was a thousand degrees in the small conference room.

"I'm sure you guys have already seen FBI Special Agents Jeremy Stitts and Chase Adams hanging around the last day or two, but I'm here now to formally introduce them."

Chase glanced around the room, remembering the time when agent Martinez and Chief Downs had embarrassed her in front of a group of men such as these back in Anchorage. But for all his faults, Detective Marsh was no Chief Downs; there was no way that the former would stand for that kind of behavior under his watch. Seated before Chase and Stitts were six detectives, who could clearly be identified by the fact that they weren't wearing uniforms, and perhaps a dozen or maybe more uniformed officers.

Detective Marsh waited for a few seconds to acknowledge them during which time Chase and Stitts nodded.

"They're here for one reason only: to help catch the bastard who's running around town slicing the throats of young women. As many of you know, or should know, despite the media lockout, this morning we discovered the body of a fourth victim: twenty-three-year-old Leah Morgan. To recap, the first three murders took place on either Friday or Saturday night, while this most recent murder came on Wednesday. The killer's speeding up, and there's no indication that he's going to stop anytime soon. Thanks to some grunt work by

Agents Adams and Stitts, we've found a link between the four women, outside of the fact that they all like to attend the downtown nightlife scene. All four of them attended a local rehab clinic for opioid abuse over the past three months called Palisades Recovery. We're trying to track down the other women who attended the center during the same time period, as well as the men, and we're also looking into the employees. I can tell you that so far, none of the names have drawn a hit in any of our databases other than for drug-related offenses."

Again, Detective Marsh paused, offering a break to allow for interruptions or questions. When none came, he continued.

"Now Agent Stitts is going to provide you with a preliminary profile of the man we're going to be looking for tonight, and every night until we catch the bastard. Agent Stitts?"

Stitts stepped forward.

"Thank you, Detective Marsh. What we're looking for is a male around the same age as the victims, but who could be as old as thirty or thirty-five if he looks young. He's going to be handsome, better than average looking, but not so good-looking that he stands out in a crowd. He's going to have a way with women, will be able to talk to them, charm them, without raising any sort of alarms. Given the proximity of the women's houses to the bars, and the fact that they all lived alone, he might be scoping out his victims beforehand, or he might just have gotten lucky," Stitts said, looking over at Chase as he spoke. "Based on the coroner's report, we know that all girls had traces of opioids in their system at the time of their deaths, and thus it's likely that our unknown subject—unsub—is targeting these women based on their addiction. Pay particularly close attention to men who appear to be moving product in the club. We also know that the unsub has consensual sex with the victims and uses a condom that he's left behind at three of the four crime scenes. After they're dead, he violates the victims with a bottle, and then duct tapes their mouths and props their eyes open with matchsticks. I will stress that this is just a profile, and it may or may not fit the description of our actual unsub. I hope that this profile can help narrow your focus, but it is important not to get tunnel vision. Keep your eyes open for everything and anything."

Stitts paused to allow this information to sink in, during which time a young detective raised his hand.

"Any idea what's with the duct tape? The matchsticks?"

Detective Marsh shook his head.

"No; as of yet, we have not determined the significance, if any, of these items. It is also unclear whether the women willingly took the heroin, or if the killer injected them with it to keep them subdued."

"What about the murder weapon? Anything special about it?" the same detective followed-up.

"All four victims were killed with a different knife, but we found knives missing from sets in three of the girls' houses that match the wounds. It's safe to assume, at this point, that the killer is using knives from the victims' houses but is bringing the matchsticks and duct tape with him to the scene. Oh, and one more thing: the clothes that the girls were wearing on the night they were murdered are missing. It is our belief that he is taking the clothes as a sort of trophy."

Stitts nodded and stepped forward again.

"Right, but we shouldn't get hung up on all of these details. Understanding the meaning behind these items, or the motives of the killer, are not necessary to find our unsub before he strikes again. Like I alluded to before, these things might have significance, or they might just be a ploy to throw us off a trail or to confuse us. Nevertheless, Agent Adams and I are looking into all of these details, but the best thing we can do now is to simply catch the unsub first and figure out the details later. The good news is that our unsub only seems to be targeting Caucasian women with dark hair from the local bar scene, particularly Club 101 and O'Cooper's Crown, who live within walking distance."

"That's right," Marsh continued. "Which is why we are going undercover at both locations, Club 101 and O'Cooper's Crown, every night until we catch this bastard. We'll have three men in the pub—Timmons, Blake, Radish—and two men in the club—Boraine and Clifton. Agent Adams here will also be undercover in the club. The rest of you are either gonna be here at the station, or at a post nearby. I've got a tech guy coming up to get everyone wired for sound and if all goes according to plan, we'll roll out tonight around nine, nine-thirty. What I can't stress enough, however, is that while we're all excited to catch this guy, we can't jump the gun on this one. Don't do a thing unless I give the go ahead. We've done a pretty good job of keeping the media at bay so far, and I've got the major outlets holding back for now, but independent sources and blogs are already starting to post information about the victims. It's only a matter of time before this thing blows up in our faces."

"And if our unsub catches wind of us and moves on, stopping him is going to be next to impossible," Stitts confirmed.

Murmuring broke out among the detectives, and Chase scratched her arm absently while she waited for the questions to come.

"About the rehab... do we think that the girls are looking to score? Is that why they're going out to the clubs? I mean, did they complete their treatment? Are they clean?" a man who identified himself as Detective Blake asked.

Chase nodded and took the opportunity to speak up.

"The director of the treatment center was less than forthcoming with details about the patients or their treatments. To be blunt, we don't know for sure. However, based on the information from friends and family of the victims, we are proceeding under the pretense that our victims have yet to relapse before meeting our unsub."

"What about fingerprints? Any fingerprints on the scene?" a uniformed officer asked.

"No; the tape was wiped clean," Marsh answered. "Any more questions before I send you clowns home to put on something that doesn't look and smell exactly like a cop?"

When no other hands were raised, Marsh checked his watch and said, "Then go home. It's seven-thirty now, be back here before nine, so that we can get wired for sound and head out for nine-thirty, *capiche*?"

Chapter 31

"I WISH YOU'D STOP looking at me like that," Chase said. "Good lord, I'm beginning to think that you're the fucking creeper."

Stitts stopped adjusting the mic that was buried inside the lapel of her dark-colored blouse that plunged a little bit too low for her liking and took a step back.

"Sorry... shit, you sure you are ready for this, Chase? I mean, after what happened with Martinez..."

Chase shook her head.

"The only thing I'm not okay with is how goddamn tight this skirt is on my ass."

She had hoped to get a chuckle out of Stitts, but he didn't even blink. The man was indeed becoming more difficult to read.

Because Chase hadn't been able to stop at her apartment in Quantico to grab her clothes—*thanks, Stitts*—she'd had to borrow something from one of the detective's wives. Unknown to her, however, was that the men of Chicago preferred their women wafer thin. Chase squatted and flexed a little, then peeled the fabric that hugged her upper thighs. She herself was a petite woman, but Detective Timmons's wife would have given Tyrion Lannister a run for his money.

"I'll be fine, Stitts. This guy hasn't been shown to be aggressive in any way until he gets the victims back to their house."

Stitts took another step backward just as Detective Marsh entered the room.

"Yeah? And what happens when he wants to go back to your place, huh? What will you do then?"

Chase offered a sly grin and then reached out and slapped Stitts on the shoulder.

"That's where you come in, Daddy."

Stitts frowned and looked as if he were about to say something when Detective Marsh broke in.

"You guys almost ready? I'll brief you on what the mobile command center's gonna look like, and what to say if you're in any trouble at all."

Chase nodded but was dismayed when she saw that Stitts was still looking at her with a strange expression on his face.

Was he staring at the inside of my forearm?

Chase had managed to borrow some concealer along with the outfit, and until now, had thought that she'd done a good job of covering up the bruising on the inside of her elbow.

No, he hadn't seen that. He didn't know about that.

"Come on, Stitts. Let's go get this bastard."

***

Anywhere between twenty and fifty people, Barney Redman had told Chase and Stitts earlier in the day. Seeing that there were at least thirty people waiting in line outside Club 101 just before ten, however, Chase was starting to seriously doubt the man's ability to count that high.

Still, this bode well for Chase and the team. The more people at the club, the more women, the more likely that their unsub would come out of hiding.

The bouncer let Chase skip the line, along with the two detectives who, to Detective Marsh's dismay, could have just as well been wearing a sandwich board that shouted, *Head's Up, Undercover Officers Approaching.* In less than five minutes, Chase found herself back in the sour-smelling place she had been earlier that day. Only this time, she didn't have her pistol with her or Agent Stitts at her side. Although she would have preferred him over Detective Boraine *and* Clifton, Detective Marsh thought it would be better served if he stayed at the command center to help coordinate both teams at the two different locations.

And yet, Chase didn't feel nervous, not quite. On the contrary, with the music blasting and the bright lights flickering above, she felt strangely energized.

Part of her knew that a crash was inevitable, her experience with heroin and emotion had told her as much, and besides, the methadone was starting to wear off, but she wanted to take advantage of this moment, hold it, for as long as she could.

Without thinking, she reached over and tapped Detective Clifton on the shoulder. The man nearly jumped out of his skin and Chase chuckled.

"I'm going to grab a drink from the bar, you guys want anything?"

Detective Clifton stared at her for a moment, clearly trying to figure out if she was serious or not.

Chase looked around, indicating the lights and the music with several waves of her hand.

"It's a club for Christ's sake, you're going to look out of place if you don't have at least one drink in your hand."

Clifton remained silent, but Detective Boraine looked over at her and said over the music, "I'll have a beer."

Rather than wait for Clifton to find his tongue, Chase made a beeline towards the bar.

She'd been wrong; although the line outside was substantial, there were only half as many people inside the bar itself. Clearly, the bouncers were trying to build up the hype by keeping people outside, making it look like Club 101 was the most popular joint in town.

As she approached the bar, Chase said a silent prayer that Barney Redman wasn't manning it.

He wasn't.

Instead, a young blond man sidled over and first took in the entire length of her body before saying anything.

Detective Marsh had made the executive decision not to contact Bruce Ibsen or the owner of O'Cooper's Crown about them going undercover, deciding that the fewer people who knew about the operation, the better.

Now, with the bartender leering at her as he was, Chase was left wondering if that had been the right decision.

"I'll take two Bud," she said with a frown.

"You sure? Our special of the night is two-for-one Crantinis, but only until midnight."

"Just give me the beers," Chase replied.

The man pouted childishly but turned his back to her to grab the bottles from the fridge. As he did, Chase reached into her purse.

And then she froze.

There, at the bottom, beside her wallet and the rolled up hundred-dollar bill, was a half-filled syringe.

Chapter 32

A HAND CAME DOWN on Chase's shoulder, and she yelped.

"Easy now, it's just me, Detective Clifton."

Chase whipped her head around to confirm that what the man was saying was true, and immediately snapped her purse shut.

Detective Clifton turned his eyes to the bartender next.

"This guy giving you a hard time?"

Before Chase could answer, the bartender spoke up.

"Me? Me?" he said in a shrill voice. "This bitch orders two beers, and I've been asking her to pay for like three minutes, but she just stares into her purse as if she's gone retarded or something."

Clifton's face twisted into a frown.

"Bitch? Watch your—"

Chase finally came to and realized what was going on.

Why the hell does every man think that I need protecting?

"It's okay, Clifton, it's fine. I got this."

She turned her body sideways and was about to reach into her purse again when Clifton nudged her arm.

"Where does this guy—"

Chase squeezed his forearm tightly.

"I got this," she hissed.

Then, without another word, she opened her purse an inch and stared inside.

The syringe was gone.

At first, Chase was shocked, but she soon realized that it had never been there in the first place.

She'd imagined it.

The hundred-dollar bill, on the other hand, was still there, but she scrounged around until she found a ten next to a tube of lipstick. She brought it out and put it on the bar, and then grabbed her beers.

"Thanks for the tip," the man spat.

Chase ignored him and spun Boraine around as she handed him a bottle.

"I should get Barney, he'll show you what's up," the bartender grumbled under his breath.

Chase pictured the man with the baseball bat, his wide-set eyes glaring. Then she saw him for what he really was a moment later, palms up, even though her gun had long since been tucked away.

Chase and Clifton moved away from the bar, and when she was confident that they wouldn't be overheard with the loud music, she addressed the detective.

"The fuck were you thinking? You were going to blow our cover already?"

Clifton shrugged, and his face turned red. Shaking her head, Chase took a large swig of her beer. It felt good in her throat, and even better in her stomach. She took another gulp, and then a third, and by this point, it was nearly half gone. Clifton took a sip of his own, but Chase, still shaking her head, snatched it from him.

"Yeah, I'm thinking that this will only cloud your already suspect judgment," she snapped.

The next two hours went by so completely uneventfully that Chase almost fell asleep three times. She thought that perhaps it was the alcohol—she had drunk her beer and Clifton's, and then ordered two more which she had promptly finished—or maybe that it was just fatigue catching up with her.

She'd been hit on three or four times, but the men who'd approached her had been harmless and were quick to take a hint. She made a mental note of their appearance and then shook her head when Clifton silently asked if he should go after them.

The man was nothing if not eager.

But other than this handful of occurrences, Chase noted nothing out of the ordinary. All told, Chase spent close to five hours inside the club, listening to music that hurt her head, swaying to the beat, trying simultaneously to look sexy and vulnerable.

This is fucking pathetic, she thought. I'm *fucking pathetic.*

As the crowd thinned and the few remaining patrons were so drunk that they could barely stand, it became clear that whatever their unsub was, he wasn't going to strike tonight. At least not here, at least not in the club with Chase.

She reached over and tapped Clifton on the shoulder.

"I think that's it, I think we should—"

Clifton, who was leaning close to her, suddenly pulled away and put two fingers to his ear. His expression quickly transitioned into a mixture of fear and excitement.

"What?" Chase asked. "What's going on?"

Although she had been wired to transmit sound, it had been impossible for Chase to be fitted with an earpiece without it looking like she was trying to sell life insurance over the phone. And now she felt out of the loop.

Clifton shushed her and waved his hand, clearly trying to hear whatever was being said through the earpiece over the bass-line that thrummed from hidden speakers overhead.

"What?" Chase asked when Clifton pulled his fingers away from his ear. "What's happening?"

Clifton's eyes nearly bugged out of his head as he turned to face her.

"We caught the guy. Holy fuck, Chase, we caught the guy!"

Chapter 33

CHASE REMAINED CALM AS she made her way out of the club, but she couldn't say the same about detectives Boraine and Clifton. The two were practically sprinting toward the front doors, which made Chase nervous.

Is this the first unsub they'd ever apprehended? Is this the first time that an undercover sting has actually worked?

"Slow down," she grumbled under her breath.

The two detectives made it outside first, not even bothering to hold the doors open for her.

For once, there was something more important than their male chauvinism.

Chase exited into the cool night air and was surprised to see that the sky was alight with the characteristic red and blue glow from police lights.

The lights and commotion had drawn a crowd, most of whom had either just vacated the bar scene or were trying to jam into one of the four restaurants in the area to get something to eat. As Chase pushed her way through the throng, to the chagrin of those inflicted by morbid curiosity to get close enough to snap a picture for their Instagram accounts, she felt a frown begin to form on her face. It wasn't a pride issue, she didn't care that she hadn't been the one to catch the unsub responsible for the murders—the only thing Chase cared about was ensuring that they stopped—but she wasn't a fan of all this pomp and circumstance.

It wasn't just memories of the crowds from the crime scenes in New York, either, the screaming women who had been calling for her head. It was the entire commercialization of criminals and criminality, the turning of what had once been considered infamy into bona fide fame. It was this sort of shit—the lights, the sirens, the crowds—this glorification, that inveigled desperate, lonely women to wed men—horrible men—on death row.

Chase was a staunch believer that it should be illegal to post the names and photos of convicted felons. Post a picture of Larry Nassar to your Instagram? A fine should be levied. Post a complimentary comment on Facebook about Bruce McArthur? *Fine.* It didn't make sense that while it was illegal for convicted criminals to profit from their crimes, others could do so without limitation.

"Out of the way," Chase grumbled, using her elbows to force her way forward. "Get the hell out of the way."

Eventually, she made her way to the front of the crowd, only to be stopped by two uniformed police officers who didn't recognize her.

"Sorry, ma'am," one of them said, deliberately avoiding eye contact. He crossed his arms over his chest in a comically cliched gesture. "You can't come through here."

Chase's scowl deepened.

"I'm FBI," she hissed, still cognizant of the people around her. Until the unsub was behind bars, she didn't want to risk her cover being blown. "Let me through."

The police officer lowered his gaze and looked her up and down. When he was done, a smirk appeared on his clean-shaven face.

"Yeah right, hon. And I'm the Queen of Canada."

"Canada doesn't have a queen, dumbass."

The police officer stopped smiling, and he raised a hand, effectively shielding Chase's face, and it was all she could do to stop from swatting it away.

"Move along now. Move along, pretty lady."

Fury building inside her, Chase tried to at least peer around the man's hand. Behind the makeshift barricade, she spotted Detective Marsh leading another man, someone she didn't recognize, with his hands cuffed behind his back, his head low, toward a white van. Behind them, she located Agent Stitts.

"Agent Stitts," she hollered. "Agent Stitts, over here!"

The crowd noticed the cuffed suspect the same time that Chase did and responded with a series of shouts and catcalls.

Shit. There's no way he's going to hear me over this crowd.

"Stitts!" Chase shouted, waving her arm at the same time.

Stitts stopped and put a finger to his ear. It was only then that Chase remembered her mic and she spoke into her blouse.

"Stitts, I'm trapped by these douchebag officers. I'm to your right, waving my hand."

Stitts looked around, and then his eyes went wide when he spotted her. He strode over, roughly pushing his way past the police officer with whom Chase had just spoken.

"What the hell are you doing over there?" And then, without waiting for a response, he said to the officer, "Let her through, let her through."

The officer stepped aside, his face turning ashen.

"Thanks," Chase grumbled, glaring at the clean-shaven man as she passed.

As the two of them hurried toward the suspect who was just being loaded into the white van, Chase turned to Stitts and said, "Well, what've we got? Is this our guy?"

Chapter 34

"HOW DO WE HANDLE this?" Detective Marsh asked.

Chase surveyed their suspect from the other side of the one-way glass.

Jason Portman was twenty-four years old and had a history of assaulting women—his previous girlfriend, and long before that, his mother of all people—and was most definitely handsome. He had jet-black hair, cropped short at the sides and longer on top, a square jaw, two days' worth of a beard, and green eyes that sparkled.

As for the charm part, however…

"I want my fucking lawyer!" the man screamed, from behind the glass. His face twisted into a grimace, and he tried with all his might to pull his arms away from the metal table. Problem was, Jason was chained to it, and his efforts only served to strain and redden his wrists.

"How long will it take for DNA to come back from the buccal swab?" Stitts asked.

Detective Marsh moved his head from side to side.

"Ten hours, maybe eight if we're lucky, more if we aren't."

Stitts appeared to mull this over.

"We can keep him for seventy-two," Marsh continued. "But we have to wait for his lawyer before we can speak to him."

"And his lawyer… you know the man?"

Detective Marsh nodded.

"Sneebly little fucker by the name of Weinberg. Slimy as they come. Bad, even by lawyer standards."

"When he was arrested for assaulting his girlfriend," Chase began, eyes still locked on Jason, "were you or any of your other men around? Have you spoken to him before?"

"No, it wasn't at our precinct. According to his parole officer, he doesn't even live in this part of town. Lives in the Cicero, about ten miles from here."

Chase raised an eyebrow.

"He's still on parole?"

Detective Marsh passed a folder to her. She opened it and scanned the first page. Jason Portman had received three months in county, three months of community service, and a three-year parole sentence for punching his girlfriend in the face. Chase briefly looked at the address, but not being familiar with Chicago, she took Detective Marsh's word on the location. The next picture was Jason's mug shot, and while there was no denying that he was a handsome man, his face was twisted into a horrible sneer not unlike the one that he was sporting at the present moment. The next photograph was of his girlfriend at the time, Tricia Wright-Monroe.

"She's blond," Chase commented as she tapped the woman's image. "And she's also a buck eighty, at least."

Detective Marsh looked over at her.

"So?"

"So, she doesn't fit the profile," Chase said.

"*Her* profile? I thought we were profiling *him*," Detective Marsh remarked, pointing at Jason Portman on the other side of the glass.

"We are," Stitts answered. "But most serials have a specific type and don't stray much. Based on the four victims, I'd say his type is a young, twenty-year-old girl with black hair, pale features, weighing anywhere between one-hundred and ten and one-hundred and thirty pounds."

"So, you're saying that because our guy's girlfriend had a little meat on her bones and bleached her hair, that this prick Jason Portman is not our guy?"

Chase didn't care for the anger that started to creep into Marsh's voice. Anger made people do stupid things, and when you did stupid things and there was a serial killer involved, people got hurt.

"What I'm saying," Chase began, struggling to keep herself calm, "is that his girlfriend, who he admitted to beating up, doesn't fit the profile of the four victims. And the MO doesn't match either. I'm not saying he isn't our guy, just stated an observation."

Despite her attempts to be cordial, Detective Marsh's face continued to redden.

"What do you mean, the MO doesn't match?" he snapped.

Chase tapped the photograph again.

"Jason Portman punched his girlfriend; there were no signs of blunt force trauma to any of the four victims. Look at his knuckles… see that, the way they're cracked? This man likes to punch things, not use a knife."

Detective Marsh's gray eyes bulged.

"That fucking prick there," he hissed, pointing at Jason again. "My guys overheard him threatening to jam a goddamn bottle up a—" Detective Marsh took a deep breath before continuing. "He threatened to violate a woman who, by the way, fits your 'profile.'"

"Just look at the fucking picture!" Chase snapped. "This guy—"

Stitts quickly stepped between them.

"Agent Adams is not saying that this isn't our guy, Bert, just that we should be cautious here. We should continue to have detectives on the street, and if this bleeds into tomorrow, we need to keep them at the clubs just to be sure. Once we get the DNA results back we'll be able to formalize the charges, but until then we play this like we're still looking for the unsub. But you know that already, Marsh. We all want to catch this guy—but we need to keep our heads about it."

Even though Stitts had said essentially the same thing that Chase had just a few moments ago, the man's words seemed to calm Detective Marsh. He hadn't come down completely but was nearly halfway there.

"Yeah, well, we're not gonna be able to do anything with Jason Portman. Not until his lawyer comes."

Chase checked her watch. It was closing in on 3:30 in the morning and she was feeling jittery, lightheaded even.

"What are the chances that he comes tonight?"

"Who? Weinburg? Ah, I give that between a zero and never chance," Detective Marsh replied. "Like I said, the guy's a fucking scumbag."

Chase rubbed her eyes.

"All right then, I'm going to go check-in to the hotel. See if I can get some shut eye."

"I'll come with you," Stitts offered.

Chase nodded, and as she did her eyes focused on Jason Portman, his face still twisted in that awful sneer.

Did you do this to those women? Did you violate them, then slit their throats?

Despite what she had said to Marsh, the man *was* angry. Very angry. And in her experience, angry people did angry things.

Chapter 35

THE HOTEL THAT STITTS and Adams were set up in was somewhere between the roach motel in Alaska and the *W* in Boston, which suited Chase just fine.

What she didn't like, however, was the fact that Agent Stitts insisted on them sharing a room. It wasn't that she was concerned that he might try something—if he'd wanted to take advantage of her, he would've done so on one of the two occasions that he had broken into her apartment—but she just wanted to be alone.

In truth, what Chase really wanted was to be alone and back in Quantico, in her room, with the stash beneath her bed…

"Up for a nightcap?" Stitts asked as he made his way over to the mini fridge. "It's on the United States of America."

Chase was too tired to have a drink. And besides, she had already had a half dozen.

"I'm all right, just want to hit the sack. I saw the way you were looking at me earlier… think I can trust you to keep your back turned while I get undressed?"

Stitts's ears reddened, but he didn't reply as he prepared himself a drink, back turned as asked.

Chase stripped down to her underwear. Normally, she slept in her underwear, but given the fact that Stitts was going to be staying in the room with her, she would have preferred to put on something else. That was impossible though, given that Stitts hadn't allowed her to go back to her room and pack anything.

Like her heroin.

"You keep your back turned, perv," Chase said as she hopped into her bed and pulled up the covers. It was strange, being in the same bedroom with another man. The only other time she had slept in the same room with someone other than her husband for as long as she could remember had been with the psychopath Chris Martinez.

And Chase couldn't shake the feeling that the reason why Stitts had insisted on this arrangement was because he was babysitting her. If it had been a money issue, then he wouldn't have been indulging on fifteen-dollar scotch minis from the fridge.

Chase tried to force these thoughts from her mind, tried to calm herself so that she could get some much-needed sleep. Her only wish was that when sleep came, it did so alone.

Without nightmares, without memories. But this was a fool's game, she knew. Only heroin could accomplish that.

"So, you think he did it?" Chase asked, knowing that the comment was clichéd, but she felt the need to fill the silence and postpone sleep if only for a few more minutes. "Jason Portman… is he our guy?"

Stitts swirled the copper-colored liquid in his glass, and then looked up at her.

"I don't know," he said simply.

Chase smirked.

"What's your gut telling you?" she asked, turning the man's words against him.

Stitts took a sip of his drink, and then glanced away.

"You're the one with the magic voodoo, why don't you tell me?"

Even though he hadn't answered the question, him throwing it back at her was answer enough.

"Me neither," Chase said as she turned onto her side.

Sleep came faster than she would've imagined, and when it did, it brought its friends.

Chapter 36

CHASE FOUND HER SISTER *sitting on a stump in the shade cast by a small barn.*

"Georgie! What's wrong with you! You can't be running off like that!"

Georgie lifted her face to look at Chase. Her lips and a good portion of her cheeks were smeared with blue.

"I was so hot!" *she said defensively.* "And I told you I was coming here."

Chase strode forward, scrunching her nose at the smell of animal dung.

"No, you didn't! Mom told you to stay by my side!"

"Yes, I did! I said I was going to find shade."

Chase sighed.

"Well, darn it, couldn't you find somewhere that didn't smell like poo?"

Georgie chuckled, and Chase shook her head.

"It's not funny. I was worried."

With a sigh, Chase reached down and patted her sister on the head.

"Come on, let's get out of here, it stinks."

Georgie slurped her snow cone, which Chase saw was mostly melted now and running down her knuckles.

With another, exasperated breath, Chase led her sister around the side of the barn.

"Let's just stick together—" *Chase started, but then immediately stopped speaking.*

There, not twenty feet from where they stood, was their mother.

Kerry Adams was leaning against a small hut, her head thrown back, her eyes closed. There was a man pressed up against her, a man wearing a white suit.

And there was only one man who Chase had ever met who wore a white suit.

The mayor.

And he was kissing Kerry. He was kissing her neck, her cheeks, her mouth, and his hands… his hands were groping her long, brown legs.

"What?" Georgie asked. "What did you say?"

Chase stepped backward, and almost bowled her sister over in the process.

"Go back, go the other way," she ordered in a dry voice.

And yet, no matter how hard she tried, Chase couldn't take her eyes away from her mother's face, the way her lips were parted ever so slightly.

Why is the mayor kissing mommy?

"Why? I thought you said —"

"Just go back," Chase hissed. She stepped toward the shade of the barn, this time pushing Georgie out of the way first.

Georgie cried out, and when her mother's eyes snapped open, Chase hurried back into the shade and out of sight.

"Why'd you do that?" Georgie whined.

"Sorry," Chase mumbled. "Let's just go this way, okay?"

Georgie had dropped what was left of her snow cone and it lay in a puddle on the ground like a melted Smurf.

"But my snow cone! I wasn't done yet!"

Chase looked down at her own snow cone. All of a sudden, the thought of even another lick of the sugary ice made her feel sick to her stomach.

"Take mine," she said.

Georgie's face lit up and she didn't need to be asked twice. When Chase, feeling lightheaded now, moved her sister toward the other end of the barn, the way they'd come, she no longer resisted.

They walked back toward the creepy snow cone vendor, but one look at the man leaning out the window with his hairy arms, and Chase turned the other way.

Dad will know what to do, *she thought.*

It took her about five minutes—five minutes of melting in the sweltering sun—to find the carnival game with the basket and the softballs that she'd spent all her allowance on.

Only her father wasn't there. The man in the straw hat was still there, still drinking from the same red plastic cup, but Keith Adams was nowhere in sight.

Chase strode toward the man.

"Back to try again?" he asked with a smirk. "I'll give you a hint, sweetheart—"

"Have you seen my dad?" Chase asked. Mother had told her not to be rude, not to interrupt, but she was too hot to be worried about that sort of thing now.

All she wanted was to get out of the sun and away from the images of her mother, with her head thrown back, the mayor running his hand…

"Who?" the man asked.

"My dad… Keith Adams." When nothing close to recognition crossed over the man's sunburnt face, Chase continued. "He was drinking with you a few minutes ago…"

The carny bit a dirty fingernail.

"Keith Adams… Keith Adams… Ah, yes! He was here, but he went home."

"Went home? Why would he go home without us?"

Georgie pulled on Chase's arm and said something, but she ignored her sister.

The man shrugged. He pulled a pack of Marlboros from his breast pocket and put one in his mouth.

"Yeah. That way."

"But why would he—"

The man lit his cigarette and exhaled a thick cloud of smoke.

"Listen, kid, if you ain't gonna play, then you gotta move along."

"But—"

The man turned his back to them.

"Move along, kid."

Chase gaped, and Georgie pulled her hand again. She turned to look at her sister, who now had purple smears across her face instead of just blue and red. Her hand was a sticky mess.

"I'm hot," she whined.

"Me too."

Chase looked in the direction that the man with the dirty nails had pointed.

"Let's go, then," she said.

Georgie, despite her complaints, resisted.

"What about Mommy? Let's go find Mommy."

An image of her mother's face flashed in Chase's mind.

"No," she said simply. "We're walking."

"But it's sooooo hot…"

Chapter 37

"IT'S OKAY, JESUS, CHASE, it's okay."

Hands gripped her shoulders and shook Chase until her eyes opened. Her scream transitioned into a gasp that caught in her throat.

It was as if her lungs had deflated, and her throat collapsed, making it impossible to suck in a breath.

"Breathe," Stitts ordered as if she didn't know what she was supposed to do. "Breathe, goddammit."

Stitts helped her into a seated position, and her lungs finally inflated. Chase croaked as she inhaled sharply.

"You scared me," he said. "What happened?"

Chase wiped the tears from her eyes with the back of her hand.

"A nightmare, just a nightmare."

Stitts stood, and she was surprised to see that he was fully dressed.

"Martinez?" he asked.

"Yeah," Chase lied. "Why are you dressed?"

"Got a call from Marsh."

The last vestiges of the horrible nightmare vanished from Chase's memory, and she swung her feet over the side of the bed, noticing, but not caring, that she was only wearing her underwear.

"What happened? Is it Jason? Is it Jason Portman?"

Stitts nodded and adjusted his tie.

"Yeah, it's Jason. And while it pains me to say it, you were right."

***

It wasn't quite eight a.m. when Stitts and Adams arrived at the precinct. It was starting out as a gray day, one where the sky was the exact same color as the clouds, which felt to Chase like an oppressive canopy pressing down on her.

The itching had returned in full force, and her mouth was so dry that it felt as if she'd gnashed mothballs for breakfast. And this wasn't the worst of it; her head was throbbing, and every movement exacerbated her headache as if she had a raw nerve exposed in every one of her teeth.

It wasn't quite eight yet, and already it was shaping up to be a horrible day.

Detective Marsh met them not ten feet inside the entrance of the police station.

"There's the little fucking prick now," Marsh grumbled under his breath.

Chase raised her head, trying her best to ignore the flare of pain, and looked to her right. Jason Portman was coming toward them, only now his face wasn't etched with a grimace, but during the night it had been replaced with a shit-eating grin. At his side was a man who Chase instinctively knew to be his lawyer, even though all she had to go on was Detective Marsh's profanity-laced description.

When Jason Portman spotted them, he started to strut as if he had just won the Stanley Cup.

"See you—" Jason's lawyer, Slimeball Weinburg, squeezed his arm hard enough to silence him. But that didn't stop the man from blowing a kiss in Chase's direction.

They watched Jason leave the station, and then Detective Marsh turned to them.

"He'll be back, mark my words. This isn't the last we hear of Jason Portman. The asshole's DNA might not match this crime, but a prick like that? A prick that talks about violating women with a beer bottle? Yeah, he'll be back. I'm sure of it."

A shudder ran through Chase, one that could have just as easily been brought on by the thought of being violated by a beer bottle as her body going through withdrawal.

Either way, it was shaping up to be a really shitty day.

Marsh cleared his throat.

"There's a meeting in the conference room in ten to decide what to do next. You want to lead it, or should I?"

***

"Jason Portman's not our guy," Detective Marsh said, addressing the same group of officers and detectives who had assembled in this room not twelve hours ago. "He's excluded based on DNA results and, given that there is no other evidence at the scene, no fingerprints, we had to let him go. And he also had an alibi for the nights that Meg and Bernice were murdered—he was out of state."

Chase had to give the man credit; he had been adamant about Jason being the unsub earlier that morning and had been the one to approve bringing him in the night before. A lesser man would have thrown blame around, but Marsh did no such thing. He just swallowed the loss, the mistake, and pressed forward.

And despite their differences of opinion, she admired him for it.

"I'm also gonna spend a moment to introduce two people to you guys—*again*. This here," Marsh said sternly, indicating Agent Stitts on his right, "is FBI Special Agent Jeremy Stitts. And to my left is FBI Special Agent Chase Adams. They're here to help us, so I want your full cooperation." He let these words linger in the air for a moment, his gaze focused directly on the uniformed officer who had given Chase a hard time the night prior. "Now that we've gotten that out of the way, Detective Peres, what can you tell us about the Palisades Recovery employees?"

A nervous looking man with a thin mustache stood, a piece of paper shaking ever so slightly in his hands.

"Well, uhh, we only got to two of them."

Detective Marsh's eyes narrowed.

"Two? Of how many?"

"Fourteen—eight full-timers and six part-timers."

"And you got to two… that's it? Just two?"

Peres's Adam's apple bobbed in his throat.

"Yeah, well we got a little excited what with the—"

Marsh waved a hand dismissively.

"Get on with it. What did you find out?"

Peres swallowed again.

"Nothing—the two employees that we checked up on were men in their late fifties, and one of them was wheelchair bound."

Chase found herself shaking her head in time with Detective Marsh.

"What about the patients?"

The mention of patients reminded Chase of the folder she'd stolen from the desk when Susan Datcher's back was turned.

She thought of the names that she'd read, of Leah, Bernice, Meg, Kirsty, and all the other potential victims.

"We're on it," Peres said quietly.

"Which really means that you haven't done fuck all."

Peres had suddenly grown very interested in the tops of his shoes.

"Well, get on with it then, get out into the field. As for the rest of you, we're going to reconvene around eight, just like last night. Let's hope that our killer was on vacation and didn't see or hear about last night's Cirque du Soleil performance outside the club. Dismissed."

All but one of the officers and detectives filed out of the room. The man who stayed behind was the uniformed police officer who had stopped Chase outside the club—*move along, pretty lady*. He approached her, his eyes on the hat that he was twisting something fierce in his hands. But before he could open his mouth to say something, Detective Marsh spoke up.

"Officer Stevenson, you going to ask her out on a date or something?"

The man's eyes shot up, and his cheeks immediately turned beet red.

"No, I, uh, I just—"

"I said dismissed, Stevenson. That means get lost, beat it."

Without another word, Stevenson turned on his heels and left the conference room. The three of them waited until the door was firmly closed behind him before speaking.

"Sorry about that," Detective Marsh said. "You ready for another round of undercover tonight?"

Chase nodded.

The phone in the man's pocket started to buzz, and he quickly answered it.

"Detective Marsh." There was a short pause. "Yeah... yeah... you sure...? and this is the only place that has the matches?"

The mention of matches piqued Chase's interest. She looked over at Stitts to see if he had any insight, but her partner simply shrugged. Detective Marsh said a few more words before thanking the person on the other end of the line and hanging up the phone. Then he turned to face them.

"So, it looks like forensics managed to match the markings on the stick part of the matches to a batch that was sent to a bar in Boston. Don't ask me how they did it, but they're fairly certain that they were sent to a place called *The Farm*."

"The Farm in Boston?" Chase repeated.

Detective Marsh nodded and Chase thought about this for a moment. Boston was a long ways from Chicago and given the fact that their killer brought the tape and matches with him to the scene, but didn't bother bringing a murder weapon, she was almost positive that these matches held some meaning to him.

Which meant that The Farm was also likely important.

"I've got a couple colleagues working in Boston; I'll tell them to check the place out," Stitts said, clearly thinking along the same lines. "Hey, Bert, did you email the DNA signature off to my guy in Quantico to see if there's a match in other states?"

Detective Marsh shook his head.

"No, got mixed up with this Jason Portman thing. I'll call down to the lab now, have them fire it off right away."

"Get them to cc me on it, and I'll make sure that it gets taken care of."

Detective Marsh nodded and turned back to his phone, and Stitts looked over at her.

"You hungry? No, scratch that. You can't be hungry after that crap you ate yesterday."

Chase smirked.

"It's called shawarma, and yes, I could eat. I could eat a whole fucking cow."

Chapter 38

CHASE DIDN'T EAT AN entire cow; in fact, she opted for something healthier: a green salad with about a half-pound of bacon thrown on top. They had almost an entire day to kill before they met with Detective Marsh and his men in the evening, and during that time, Chase intended to buy something more comfortable to wear. Still slutty, still to the unsub's liking, but something that didn't hug her ass so tight that she wasn't able to fart if she needed to.

They didn't say much during lunch, and Stitts resigned himself to hanging around the background as Chase did some quick shopping. She picked up the basics—some fresh underwear, a bra, a pair of jeans, a couple of T-shirts—and of course, the outfit she planned to wear to the club when she went undercover again.

Lunch and shopping, despite detesting the latter, served at the very least to be a healthy distraction from the itching that seemed to be crawling both up and down her arm now. Her fingertips were particularly bothersome, and she noticed with chagrin that she had started to roll her fingers as if she were balling invisible pieces of string.

It was closing in on 2 p.m. when Chase was finally done, and both she and her new bodyguard/father, Jeremy Stitts, thought it best to head back to the hotel. Three times the man had asked if she was okay, if she was comfortable going undercover again, and all three times Chase had essentially told him to fuck off, although not in so many words.

Who is he to ask if I'll be okay going undercover? I was an undercover narcotics officer for six months in Seattle!

Back at their shared hotel room, Jeremy opted for a nap, and while Chase was tired, extremely tired after last night in the club and the poor quality of sleep she'd gotten in the early hours of the morning, she decided against trying to get some shut-eye.

She was afraid the dreams would come back. The dreams and the memories.

Instead, Chase stepped outside the room and found herself staring at her phone, sipping on a can of Coke. Although the day had started out dreary, the sun had decided to show its colors on several occasions.

And this was one of those occasions.

She started to flick through her photographs, staring with head tilted at the ones of her son Felix and his mop of white hair.

How long has it been since I last saw him? she wondered. Both Felix and Brad had visited her in the hospital after she'd been shot, and Brad had permitted Felix to stay with her for a weekend prior to her being shipped out to Quantico. It couldn't have been more than... what? Two months? Three at most? And yet to Chase, it felt like a year or more.

Struck by a sense of nostalgia, which in itself was strange considering she was thinking about her own son, Chase switched from the photographs to her contacts. She scrolled to Brad's name, and her finger hovered over it for a second.

Her hand was trembling so badly that when she brought the can of Coke to her lips, she nearly spilled it all over the blouse she had just purchased.

When she'd left for Quantico, she and Brad had agreed that it was in Felix's best interest if she didn't try to contact him until she got back, whenever that was. It was just too confusing for the boy to come in and out of her life like that. Right now, Mommy was away at work where they didn't have phones, and that while she loved him very much, he would have to wait for her to come back home before they spoke again.

What the fuck is wrong with me? Chase asked herself for what felt like the thousandth time. *If I want to speak to my own son, I should be able to wherever and whenever I want.*

She clicked send and chewed on her bottom lip as she waited.

Chase didn't expect her estranged husband to answer, and was surprised when a familiar voice said, "Hello?"

She choked down a mouthful of Coke.

"Brad?"

There was a long, awkward pause.

"I don't... I don't think this is a good idea, Chase," Brad said softly. "We agreed—"

Chase closed her eyes.

"I just want to talk to him. Please. I won't... I won't cause any problems."

Another pause.

"Make it quick, Chase. He's doing his homework."

Chase heard muffled voices, and then Felix came on the line.

"Hello?"

"Hi, sweetheart, it's Mommy," Chase said, wiping her nose with the back of her hand. "I miss you."

"I miss you too, Mommy. When are you coming home?"

Chase barely held back a sob. Tears had started to stream down her cheeks.

"I miss you so much, sweetie. So, so much."

"Daddy says that you're sick, Mommy."

Chase tried to get angry but couldn't do it. She was, after all, sick.

"I know," she whispered, "I'm going to get help. And then I'm going to come see you, okay?"

"Okay, Mommy... oh, Daddy says I have to finish my homework now. I love you."

"I love you, too, Felix. So very much. Just—"

But Felix was no longer on the phone.

"We gotta go, Chase. I'm sorry but—"

"Please," Chase sobbed. "Just give me another minute with him, I—"

"Chase."

"*Please.*"

"Chase, I don't think—"

"Goddamn it, Brad! All I'm asking for is—Brad? *Brad!*"

Chase pulled the phone away from her ear and stared at it. He had hung up on her. The bastard had the audacity to hang up on her when all she wanted to do was to speak to her son.

Still sobbing, Chase swore and shoved her phone back into her pocket. She turned her head skyward, but the sun had disappeared again.

Scratching furiously at the inside of her arm, Chase looked back into the hotel room. The door was still propped open, and peering inside, she could see that Stitts was on his back, snoring softly.

Without a second thought, she leaned inside the door and scooped her partner's car keys off the table.

Felix is right... he may only be eight years old, but he's right. I'm sick, Chase thought as she headed toward Stitts's rental. *But I can't do anything about that now. Right now, I need something to help me get through this, to help me catch a killer before he strikes again.*

Chapter 39

CHASE HAD NO TRUE destination, she just drove. But while she wasn't headed anywhere in particular, she had a singular goal: to score.

But Chase knew less about Chicago than she did Woodbridge or Quantico, and the idea of cruising the streets held no interest to her. The possibility of another man gripping her by the throat, even though she had her gun at the ready instead of a urine-soaked tampon, was out of the question as well.

It was, therefore, less than surprising that she found herself back at Palisades Recovery. Only this time, she didn't park in the lot out front. Instead, she circled around the back of the building and waited.

When she had gripped Craig by the collar yesterday and pulled him close, she had smelled the reek of cigarettes on his breath. And judging by the pile of butts just outside the door, this was where the man came to smoke.

"C'mon, c'mon," she muttered as she scratched at her arm. Her eyes darted to the cell phone on the dash, to the door, and back again. It was only a matter of time before Stitts woke up and wondered where the fuck she and his car had gone. The last time she'd left with his vehicle, she'd come back hours later with scratches all over her throat.

"C'mon. Please."

Less than five minutes later, the door swung open and Craig wandered out into the afternoon light.

Chase took a deep breath and then silently stepped out of the car. She moved quickly across the parking lot, keeping her chin low.

Craig never saw her coming.

"Craig," Chase said when she was within six feet of the man.

His eyes shot up.

"Oh, no," he said, flicking his cigarette to the ground and reaching for the door. "Not you. You almost cost me my job—"

"Just wait, I want to talk to you."

The man shook his head violently.

"No way, if you want to talk to me, Susan said that you need to go through her. She said that—"

He started to pull the door open, and Chase stepped forward.

"I don't give a fuck what Susan says, I need to talk to you."

Craig pulled the door open and tried to slip inside, but Chase reached out and grabbed him by the collar.

"Hey!" he cried. If it hadn't been for his death grip on the door handle, she might have pulled him to the ground.

"I don't give a fuck what Susan says, I want you to tell me who your supplier is."

The man stared at her as if she'd grown a second head.

"Lady, I don't know what—"

"Don't lie to me!" Chase shrieked. "I know you're fucking cutting heroin with methadone. Just tell me *who your supplier is!"*

The man was close to tears now.

"Please, you're choking me," he gasped. Chase's hand had twisted so deeply into his collar that her fingers had turned white—the same shade as Craig's face.

"Just tell me where to get some heroin," she hissed.

The man gasped, and Chase finally let go of his collar.

"You're a fucking psycho," he wheezed. "You're a psycho bit—"

"Give me some methadone," she snapped, her hand falling to the gun on her hip. "Give me some goddamn methadone."

The man's eyes bulged when he saw the pistol.

"I—I don't have any."

"Liar!"

"No, seriously, Susan took them all after—"

Chase's phone buzzed, and she reached into her pocket and pulled it out.

It was Stitts.

"Fuck!" she swore, raising her eyes.

During the few seconds that it took her to pull out her phone, Craig had somehow managed to slip inside the partly open door. And now, through the inch-wide opening, he was aiming his cell phone at her.

"No you don't!" she raged, striding forward.

Chase heard the sound of the camera shutter seconds before the door slammed closed. She grabbed the handle and pulled, but it didn't budge.

Craig had locked it from the inside.

"Fuck!" she screamed, hammering on the door with her fist.

Chase's phone buzzed again, and she gritted her teeth in frustration.

Glancing around, she hurried back to the car and managed to slide inside before her phone stopped ringing.

After a deep, shuddering breath, she answered it.

"Chase? Where'd you run off to? It's—"

"I'll be back in ten, Stitts. I just needed to go for a drive to clear my head. Couldn't sleep."

"Alright, see you—"

Chase hung up the phone and tossed it onto the dash. As she did, her eyes passed the rearview mirror.

Chase barely recognized herself. Her eyes were red-rimmed, her hair a mess. Her skin was a pallor only seen in death.

The phone on the dash buzzed again, but she ignored it this time.

"Fuck, fuck, *fuck!*" Chase shouted, slamming her palms down on the steering wheel with every curse.

Chapter 40

THE MUSIC WAS EVEN more obnoxious on Friday night.

"Clifton, you want a drink?" Chase asked.

Detective Clifton, who seemed to be in his own world tonight, shook his head.

"Suit yourself," Chase grumbled. It was better if she drank alone, anyway; just in case the unsub was here, it was best if someone stayed sober.

The bartender was the same as the night prior, and as she approached, he gave her a sour look and immediately moved to the other end of the bar to serve a girl who was twelve if she was a day, and her boyfriend who looked about fifty.

"Oh, come on."

Holding her breath, Chase opened her purse, nervous that the phantom syringe would be there again.

It wasn't.

She reached inside and pulled out a hundred-dollar bill.

"Hey, fucktard, give me a beer and keep them coming."

The curse drew the bartender's attention, and the hundred-dollar bill kept it.

With the aid of alcohol, the music started to grow on Chase like a festering sore that had been there for some time and she was only now becoming accustomed to it.

She swayed to the beat, waving her free hand in the air above her head. For the first time since leaving Quantico, since the last time she had shot up, Chase felt free. Maybe it was the music, more likely it was the alcohol, but whatever the reason, Chase wasn't thinking about her next hit, about her sister, Agent Martinez, or being violated with a bottle and having her throat slashed—she thought of none of those things. The only thing that concerned Chase now was the music and the way it made her skin thrum.

The bass beat intensified, and Chase's hip-swaying increased with the tempo. Sweat had begun to form on her brow, in her armpits, and between her breasts, but she didn't care. She was lost, lost in her own world, in a world that wasn't fully and completely ravaged by pain.

She danced, she sipped her drink, and she never wanted this moment end.

But it had to, and when it did, Chase was pissed.

A hand came down on her shoulder, and at first, Chase thought it was someone who wanted to dance with her, and she backed into him, pressing her ass against his belt.

But then, to her dismay, the hand on her shoulder extended, pushing her away.

With a sour expression on her face, she turned and was about to scold the college kid for teasing her, when she froze.

It wasn't a collar-popping trust fund baby; it was Detective Clifton.

"You okay?" he asked, his brow furrowing. Without waiting for an answer, he added, "We just got a call. There's been a hit on the DNA. Some guy from Boston."

Chase felt momentarily dizzy and closed her eyes, trying to understand what the man was saying.

DNA hit? A man from Boston?

She took a step backward and stumbled. Detective Boraine suddenly appeared and wrapped his arm around her.

"You okay?" Detective Boraine asked.

"Why does every fucking man think he has to look after me? Always asking if I'm okay?" she slurred, moving away from the two men. "Of course I'm okay… I'm always okay."

The detectives looked at her strangely and then Clifton snapped his fingers.

"Agent Adams? Snap out of it. The gig's up. We got a hit on the DNA, a guy from Boston."

Chase started to feel sick to her stomach, and there was nothing she wanted more than to get out of this place. The music, which she had enjoyed just moments ago, now seemed like a binaural beat that was messing with her equilibrium.

"Yeah, just like the last guy? Like Jason Portman?" she said.

Detective Clifton, his face a mask of concern, reached for her, but Chase pulled away. When Detective Boraine stepped forward next, Chase was no longer in the club. Instead, she was back in the dingy crack house, and Detective Boraine was Tyler Tisdale, with his rotting teeth and foul-smelling breath. Detective Clifton was a John, a fat man with sweaty tits and a greasy mustache she had slept with for a hit.

"Get away from me," she spat. The detectives, confused now to the point of immobilization, simply stared. "Get the fuck away from me."

Chase stumbled again and nearly bowled over a young girl holding an over-sized crantini.

"Where are you going?"

"Fuck off," Chase said as she made her way towards the door.

I just need fresh air, if I get some fresh air, I'll be fine. Fresh air and something to eat, something to fill my stomach.

Chase burst into the night and forced her way through a throng of people toward the shawarma shop that she had indulged in the day prior.

Thankfully, most everyone preferred McDonald's, it appeared, and the line was short.

"I'll have a shish taouk—" Chase began, speaking slowly to avoid slurring her words. But before she could even finish her order, Chase felt eyes on her. She turned, expecting to see either Clifton or Boraine approaching, but was pleasantly surprised. A handsome man in his mid-twenties with dark black hair and a grin on his face stared back.

"Hi there," the man said softly. "You having a good night? Because I know a couple of things that can probably make it even better."

PART III - Everyone Casts a Shadow

PRESENT DAY

Chapter 41

CHASE STARED AT THE face of a serial killer and was momentarily frozen in place. She had been around murderers before, had slept with one, in fact, in the form of ex-FBI Agent Chris Martinez.

But she hadn't known Martinez was a killer until the bitter end.

When this man had touched her, however, when he had grabbed her forearm and pulled up her blouse sleeve, she'd *seen*; Chase had seen Leah Morgan's sweaty face staring back, her eyes pinched in ecstasy.

There was no doubt in her mind that this man was their killer. And yet, Chase felt unable to act, unable to do anything at all. Fear coursed through her, and when the man led her away from the shawarma shop, she felt helpless but to obey.

"My name's Frank," the man said as they walked. "Frank Carru—"

A shadow came out of nowhere and collided with Frank's side. At first, Chase thought it was just a drunken passerby who had stumbled and fallen, but when they landed in a heap on the ground, the man didn't offer an apology or even try to help Frank to his feet.

Instead, Frank's arms were yanked behind his back.

"Hey, get off him," Chase shouted, suddenly free of her paralysis. The man turned, and Chase's jaw went slack. "Stitts? What are you doing?"

Agents Stitts looked incredulous.

"Chase? What the fuck are *you* doing here?"

The man beneath Stitts started to struggle and somehow managed to crane his neck around to look up at Chase.

"Who are you people?" Frank demanded. When Stitts had taken him down, he'd smacked his nose off the pavement and twin streams of blood ran from his nostrils.

"Shut up," Stitts snapped, pushing his forearm down on the back of Frank's head, grinding his face into the pavement.

"What are you doing, Stitts?"

"You know who this is?" her partner asked. "Chase, you know who this is?"

Chase swallowed hard, wishing that she hadn't indulged in as many drinks as she had.

She knew who Frank Carruthers was, but if she needed any further confirmation than what she'd seen through the man's eyes, Stitts's next words sealed it for her.

"This is the killer," her partner whispered in an airy tone. Then, as Chase started to process this information, Stitts turned to the man on the ground. "Frank Carruthers, I'm arresting you for the murders of Bernice Wilson, Megan Docker, Kirsty Buchanan, and Leah Morgan. You have the right to remain silent. Anything you say…"

Chapter 42

"I THINK IT'S PROBABLY best if you stay here," Detective Marsh said to Chase. The three of them—Marsh, Stitts, and Chase—were back in the viewing room in the precinct, once again behind the one-way glass. Only it wasn't Jason Portman on the other side this time, but Frank Carruthers.

And unlike Jason, Frank didn't look angry; instead, he looked genuinely confused.

Confused and scared.

"I want to go in there," Chase replied. Her mind was fixated on what she'd seen when Frank had touched her arm, and now that the alcohol had all but worn off, she needed to feel him again.

Just to be absolutely certain.

Agent Stitts suddenly stepped beside her.

"I think Bert is right, you should probably stay here," he said, eying her suspiciously. She knew that Stitts wasn't buying her story, that once Detective Clifton had told her that they had gotten the DNA match, she'd abandoned the undercover operation and headed outside to grab some food. By sheer chance alone, she had identified Frank Carruthers as someone who fit the profile and was in the process of questioning him when Stitts had laid his shoulder into the man. It was a shitty lie, but it was all she could come up with at the time.

She kept what Frank had said to her, and what had happened when he'd grabbed her arm, to herself for the time being. Thankfully, there had been so much commotion at the time, that no one seemed to have overheard what had transpired between them over the mic she'd been wearing.

"You having a good night? Because I know a couple of things that can probably make it even better."

There was only one thing that could make her feel better, but the real question was, how could Frank *know*?

And until she figured that out, Chase was going to keep this part of the conversation to herself and hoped that Frank did the same.

"I think I should talk to him; he might open up seeing that I'm a woman."

Detective Marsh looked over at Stitts, and they exchanged a glance.

"We'll only use you if we have to," Agent Stitts said before he and Marsh made their way towards the door.

Chase didn't care much for Stitts's language.

… use you if we have to.

There had been someone else from her past that liked to use her, use her in ways that Chase wished she could forget.

But what choice did she have? Stitts was technically her superior and she still had a slight buzz. Besides, if she pushed too hard now, the men might become suspicious. And Stitts was already wary.

She'd get her chance, Chase knew. For now, however, she resigned herself to simply watch.

Detective Marsh approached Frank first, putting a closed manila folder on the table between them. He had a calm demeanor, which surprised Chase. Agent Stitts, on the other hand, stayed in the background, clinging to the walls like a midafternoon shadow.

"You've been advised of your rights, Frank. You know that you have the right to remain silent, and you have the right to an attorney. You've waived these rights, but at any point during this interview, you can ask for an attorney and we will stop right away. Do you understand this?"

Frank nodded.

"Are you going to tell me what this is about?" he asked, wiping his nose with the tissue that had been provided. He hooked a chin at Stitts. "This fucking guy was saying something to me outside the club, but I was too busy concentrating on my busted nose to hear."

Detective Marsh grimaced.

"We'll get to that. But let's start slow, like a first date, alright?"

Frank's dark eyebrows knitted, but he nodded.

"Good. What do you do for a living, Frank?"

"I'm a salesman. I work for Roche, sell biological consumables to hospitals and labs all over the Midwest."

Detective Marsh nodded and then he started to pace, a tried and tested technique to put the suspect on edge. As Chase watched, Frank's eyes followed Marsh about the room. It appeared as if he had completely forgotten about Agent Stitts, which was clearly by design.

"You travel a lot, Frank?"

"Yeah, gone almost every week. Back on weekends, though."

"But sometimes you're here during the week, aren't you? In Chicago?"

Frank's eyes narrowed.

"Yeah," he replied hesitantly. "Sometimes I'm here during the week, sometimes just for a few hours during a stopover or to pick up some clean clothes. Are you gonna tell me what this is about?"

Detective Marsh crossed his arms over his chest.

"Open the folder, Frank."

Frank, still suspicious, reached out and opened the folder. As he leaned forward and read, his face started to turn red with anger.

After only thirty seconds, Frank shoved the folder away from him.

"I knew this would happen," he said, shaking his head. "I knew this would happen again."

"Yeah, you can't just go around raping women and defiling them with a beer bottle and expect that to fade away from your record."

Frank's eyes shot up and he glared at Marsh.

"I was acquitted. I didn't do any of that horrible stuff," Frank snapped.

Chase raised an eyebrow; everything that had happened since her partner and the detective had entered the room was new to her. Clearly, when she'd been undercover in the club, Stitts and Marsh had discovered information about Frank Carruthers that they'd neglected to share with her.

Detective Marsh unfolded his arms.

"You got off on a technicality, Frank."

Frank shook his head.

"No... no I didn't do it. I didn't do any of what she said. I didn't rape her... Jesus Christ, I didn't do that disgusting stuff with the bottle. Shit, Rebecca was just pissed because I moved away, moved on from her psycho bullshit."

"So, what? She just made it all up?"

Frank slumped back in his chair and now it was his turn to cross his arms.

"I'm not saying she made it up—I don't know what happened to her. All I know is I didn't do it."

"You were the only other person with a key to her apartment, Frank. So, if you didn't do it, who did? You trying to tell me that she did that to herself? Is that it, Frank?"

"I dunno—you ever seen *Gone Girl*? I don't know what happened to Becca, but I didn't do it."

Chase stared at the man intently through the glass, trying to figure out if he was lying. She didn't immediately pick up on any of the common tells—fidgeting hands, averting his gaze, offering too much detail—but the best liars, and poker players, could hide these things well, she knew.

"Rebecca... she was crazy. A mental case."

Detective Marsh took a second folder from Stitts.

"She was crazy, so you made her pay, didn't you, Frank?" As he spoke, Detective Marsh collected the first folder, and replaced it with the second. Frank swallowed hard and didn't immediately move to open it. "What about Leah? Bernice and Meg? Kirsty?"

"Who?"

Detective Marsh pointed at the folder.

"Open it," he said.

Frank's Adam's apple did a little dance in his throat as he reached out with a tentative hand and pulled the cover open.

His eyes focused on the first image.

"W-What is this?" he stammered. "What the hell is this?"

"Look at the other girls," Detective Marsh ordered. When Frank's eyes remained locked on the first image, which Chase recognized as Leah Morgan's face with duct tape over her mouth, and matchsticks holding her eyes open, Marsh shouted and slammed his fists on the table. "Look at them all, Frank! Look at what *you did!*"

When Frank still did nothing, and his eyes started to water, Detective Marsh reached out and spread the images of the four victims on the table in front of them.

"Look at what you did!"

Frank's face turned gray.

"I think I'm going to be sick," he gasped. "I'm going to be sick."

Chapter 43

"WHAT A FUCKING JOKE," Detective Marsh muttered under his breath. "Those crocodile tears are so obvious that they look like they've been wrung out of a Lacoste T-shirt."

Chase, on the other hand, wasn't so sure, despite what she and Frank had exchanged less than a few hours ago. To her, the man looked genuine, and she had never heard of someone actually vomiting on command. Someone who wasn't a bulimic, that is.

And yet, she was hesitant to voice her opinion.

Even after I saw Leah's face… when Frank touched me… why am I still not convinced?

"He seems quite distraught about it," Stitts commented.

"Distraught or not, he did it. He fucking murdered those girls," Detective Marsh concluded.

The man was clearly expecting confirmation from either Chase or Stitts, but when nothing came, he felt the need to explain himself further.

"Look, Frank was arrested for raping and violating his girlfriend with a bottle and gets off on a technicality—the fact that the girl's clothes, which she claims she was wearing that night, are missing. Then, as soon as he's released, Frank takes off, flees Boston and comes here to Chicago. That was six months ago. Now we have four victims, all violated with beer bottles, and his DNA shows up at the crime scene? I tell you guys what, I may not have the experience or the intelligence of the FBI, but this is as slam dunk a case as I've ever seen."

And yet, despite the man's words, the fact that he had felt the need to recount the details, made Chase wonder if he hadn't also picked up on the strangeness of the case.

"There are some things that just don't add up," Agent Stitts mused.

"Like what?"

"Like why he would leave his DNA behind, when he knows it's on file from when he was initially arrested. And what's with the tape, the matchsticks?"

Detective Marsh shrugged.

"I'm telling you, short of a written confession or a videotape of the murders, this is as cut and dry as they come. I mean, look at him. He looks nervous as all hell, like a man who just farted in a crowded elevator. Give me ten minutes, and I'll get him to sign a goddamn confession saying he did all of it. Then he can get his fucking—"

Detective Marsh's phone buzzed, and he answered it.

"Marsh here," he said harshly.

While Marsh spoke on the phone, Chase turned her attention to Agent Stitts. The man was staring through the glass at Frank Carruthers, his lips pressed together tightly, and Chase was suddenly reminded of something that Agent Martinez had said repeatedly during their short time together.

There's not always a reason, a nice clean explanation or motive for some of the worst crimes ever committed by man.

Despite the fact that Agent Martinez was a bona fide psychopath, she knew that, in this case, the man had been right. Not all crimes *had* a nice clean motive. Applying rational thought and reasoning to irrational situations and acts just didn't work.

And yet in this case—in the case of Frank and the four dead girls—she couldn't help but think that there was an underlying motive, something that they were all overlooking. For one, why would a man as good-looking as Frank Carruthers murder these girls? Clearly, he was handsome enough, charming enough, *rich* enough to sleep with them without having to resort to trickery or drugs.

After leaving the interrogation room, Chase had been given a chance to review Frank's file. Outside of the allegations made by Rebecca Hall, Frank appeared to be a law-abiding citizen. She wasn't overlooking what Rebecca claimed the man had done, but unlike what Detective Marsh had said, it wasn't true that he'd gotten off on a technicality alone.

True, Rebecca's clothes, a key piece of evidence, had gone missing, but what Marsh neglected to mention was that Frank had an alibi: he'd been out of state on business during the time that Rebecca Hall claimed she'd been raped and mutilated by him.

The alibi had been ironclad, so much so that the DA had decided not to prosecute. And so far as Chase could tell, there had been no other suspects in the case since and not a single lead.

Detective Stitts suddenly looked up and their eyes met. For the briefest of moments, she thought she saw the man shake his head.

Stitts had become more guarded over the past week or so, but Chase thought she read the man clearly enough just then. She opened her mouth to say something, when Detective Marsh hung up his phone and turned towards them, a smug expression on his aging face.

"That was Detective Timmons. You aren't gonna believe this, but they searched Frank's house. Wanna know what they found?"

The question was rhetorical, of course, but Chase already knew the answer even if it had been legitimate.

"The girls' clothes," Detective Marsh said. "They found the victims' clothes at Frank Carruthers's house."

Chapter 44

"YOU WANT TO GO back to the hotel and get some rest?" Stitts asked.

Chase thought about this for a moment before shaking her head.

"No, not rest. I just need to shower and change. And eat; I could probably eat."

Stitts raised an eyebrow, and then he checked his watch.

"You can always eat."

"Well, you did knock my shawarma to the ground," Chase replied with a smirk.

"All right," Stitts agreed. "A shower, a couple of Advil, some hot coffee. Let's let Detective Marsh work on Frank for a bit, give him some space. The man's not going anywhere. Besides, I think it's time that we compared notes, if you know what I mean."

Chase nodded and stood, stretching her back and her hips.

"Coffee would be good… a coffee with bourbon would be better."

"Yeah, I'm thinking just plain coffee for you," Stitts said with a smile.

***

Water one degree shy of scalding cascaded over Chase's short dark hair and shoulders, slowly forming rivulets that ran between her breasts. She lowered her head and pressed her palms against the moist tile wall in front of her.

Images began to flash behind her closed lids.

She was back in Leah Morgan's apartment, only it wasn't the fourth victim's eyes that she was seeing through now, but her own.

Frank Carruthers was on top of her, slowly rocking his hips back and forth. Chase was disgusted, horrified by this, but she reached out anyway, her fingers grabbing onto Frank's flexed ass cheeks as he buried himself inside her.

Chase was disgusted, but this was slowly replaced by something else.

Pleasure.

"You like that?" Frank asked.

Chase could only moan, which encouraged him further.

Yes, she liked that; she liked that very much.

And as Frank's thrusts increased in tempo, she liked it even more.

Chase's leg muscles clenched, and her toes curled, and she let out a deep, shuddering moan. She opened her eyes then and was surprised to see that her nipples had gone hard and that her legs were bent and weak.

That her fingers had found their way to between her legs.

Her breathing was shallow and coming through pursed lips.

What the hell was that? What just happened?

She shuddered again, then took a deep breath.

Confused, Chase washed quickly and then stepped out of the shower. As she dried herself, she shouted to Stitts in the other room.

"Stitts, you still there?"

"Yeah, still here. Getting hungry, though. You almost ready?"

***

"Jesus, you eat like a trucker, anyone ever tell you that?"

Chase shoveled a spoonful of eggs and a couple of pieces of fried potatoes into her mouth.

"No one's ever dared."

Egg yolk ran down her chin, and she wiped it away with a napkin.

Stitts's upper lip curled and he pushed his bagel and cream cheese away from him, settling for a sip of coffee. Then he waited patiently for Chase to finish her meal, before opening up about what was on both of their minds.

"What did you see, Chase?" Stitts said quietly, leaning over the breakfast table.

Chase could normally hold a straight face no matter what, something she had learned very early on during her poker playing days, but after what had happened in the shower...

She blinked and knew that nothing but the truth would serve her in this situation.

"When I touched him, I saw."

Stitts nodded.

Chase expected the man to ask *what* she had seen next, but he surprised her by skirting the subject.

"Has this ever happened before? With a living person, I mean?"

Chase looked down at her coffee and took a sip before answering.

"No. Never."

And now the question will come, Chase thought. *He'll ask me what I saw, what my gut is telling me. If I think I'm going crazy.*

But Stitts didn't say anything; he simply stared at her. If there was something, *anything*, that she was certain of with Jeremy Stitts, it was that the man cared.

Cared a lot.

Too much, maybe. When you cared as much as he did, you eventually got hurt.

After the silence had dragged on for so long that it had grown uncomfortable, Stitts eventually spoke.

"Frank Carruthers has a Bachelor of Science from MIT. He's been in sales his whole life and has always been in the top five percent or so of any of the companies that he's worked for. A search of his computer pulled up nothing but some porn—normal shit—and a ton of correspondence with women. He's had a couple parking tickets, almost lost his license once for speeding, but that's it. Other than this Rebecca Hall thing, of course. And do you want to know what he sells?"

"I think he said he sells biological products to labs, or something like that."

Stitts nodded.

"Yeah, but not just *any* biological products; he sells DNA and RNA extraction kits."

Chase's frown deepened as she realized what this meant. During one of their first discussions with Detective Marsh, the idea that their unsub had been familiar with fingerprints, but not DNA, had come up.

Clearly, Frank Carruthers was well-versed in DNA.

So if you're gonna use a condom at all with girls you're about to murder, why leave it at the scene?

"Yeah, I know what you're thinking—what Marsh said. But here's the thing; the girls didn't have any STDs. All of them were clean."

Chase shook her head.

"All the girls... shit, what's the connection with Palisades, Stitts? Frank isn't an employee and was never a patient. Is it all just a coincidence?"

"I don't know. We're still trying to gain access to Frank's phone, so maybe that will help clear things up. Detective Marsh and his men are also trying to find Rebecca Hall, but so far no luck. She seems to have disappeared ever since the charges against Frank were dropped about six months ago."

Chase took another sip of her coffee and tapped her finger against the porcelain.

"What's his motive? I get it, you don't always have to have one, but the matchsticks? Tape? Heroin? What's going on here, Stitts?"

The man's face was smooth, flaccid.

"I don't know, Chase. I thought maybe you could help me with that part."

Chase looked down and took a deep breath.

"When Frank touched me... I saw the same thing as when I touched Leah. They were... *intimate*, but there was no fear. I felt that—" *he was the killer; in fact, I was convinced that when he looked at me, Frank was the serial killer we're looking for,* "—they were happy. But there was something else, something that just didn't fit."

She paused, trying to think back to the first vision she'd had back at Leah's apartment.

"What is it, Chase? What did you see?"

Chase shuddered.

"There was a shadow there, like someone was watching. I know it sounds crazy, but..." she let her sentence trail off.

Stitts didn't push her any further, which was a good thing because Chase had come to her wit's end. She didn't want to relive any of her visions that contained Frank Carruthers.

They finished their coffee in silence, and before Stitts asked for the check, he looked up at her.

"I think you're right," he said.

Chase raised an eyebrow.

"About what?"

"That we should've had some bourbon in our coffee."

Chapter 45

DESPITE DETECTIVE MARSH'S CLAIM, not only had Frank Carruthers not cracked, but his story seemed to become more solid as the afternoon bore on.

And the presence of his lawyer wasn't helping any.

"We know you did it, Frank. We had the stomach contents of the victims examined—we know that you went on the prowl at night, after the bars closed, and picked up the girls outside the shawarma joint. We know that you went back to their place and had sex with them. But that wasn't enough for you, was it? No, not by a long shot. You drugged them next, then raped them with a beer bottle. And yet you still weren't satisfied. You had to end it. These poor girls—Leah Morgan, Meg Docker, Kirsty Buchanan, and Bernice Wilson—poor, beautiful girls, dead. You slit their throats. Only then were you done. Until the next victim, of course."

Frank stared at his hands as the detective spoke.

"I thought you said Gwen," he said in a calm tone.

"Gwen? Who's that? Another one of your victims?"

The name seemed oddly familiar to Chase as if she'd heard it not that long ago, but she couldn't place it.

"I told you, I didn't do anything."

At this point, Frank's lawyer leaned over and whispered something into his client's ear.

Frank turned back to Detective Marsh.

"I didn't even know they were dead," he whispered, his eyes locked on his hands again. "I swear, I didn't know they were dead. I'm not much for the newspaper or the news in general, and I travel a lot. I didn't know."

Detective Marsh smirked.

"Yeah, sure, just like your next victim wasn't going to be the hot little brunette with the nice rack."

Chase stiffened at the callousness of Marsh's words, but Stitts rested a hand on her shoulder to reassure her that the man knew what he was doing.

"I bet you didn't count on her being an FBI Agent, did you? Hell, now that I see how unremorseful you truly are, I'm not sure you'd even care. Shit, I think you might have even wanted to get caught," Marsh continued.

The lawyer whispered something else into Frank's ear, and the man nodded before replying.

"I already admitted to having sex with these girls—with Bernice, Meg, Leah, Kirsty, as well as Gwen and Tiffany—but I swear, what we did was fully consensual. I told you already, I'm usually only home for a few days on the weekend, and I... well, you know."

Marsh shook his head.

"'Fraid I don't know. The only thing I know is that you've admitted to having sex with all of the victims and their clothes, the clothes that they were wearing on the night they were killed, were found in your house. But no, I don't know nothing about the sick shit you're into."

Frank suddenly rubbed his temples as if a migraine had come on.

"My client has been nothing but cooperative at this point," the lawyer interjected. "I don't think..."

Chase looked away for a moment and tried to concentrate.

Bernice, Meg, Leah, Kirsty, Gwen, and Tiffany...

The last two names weren't part of the investigation, but they seemed familiar to Chase.

"Bingo," she whispered, snapping her fingers.

Stitts looked over at her.

"What? What is it?"

Chase's eyes moved about the room, and she grabbed the first folder that she saw.

It was the one with pictures of the four victims that Marsh had first shown Frank. She grabbed the one beneath it, which turned out to be the police report from Frank's prior arrest.

"Chase? What are you looking for?"

"The sheet... the patient sheet from Palisades."

Stitts scrounged through a pile of papers before coming up with it.

"Here," he said, and Chase snatched it from him and quickly scanned the list.

Her eyes skipped over Leah Morgan's name, and the names of the other victims.

"There," she said, pointing at a name and showing it to Stitts.

"Gwen Palovniak," Stitts said.

Chase nodded and moved her finger down several lines.

"And here, look: Tiffany McDavid."

Stitts scratched his chin and shook his head at the same time.

"There's no way that it's a coincidence. He's targeting them from the clinic."

"No shit," Chase replied.

Stitts stared at her for a second before nodding. Then he reached over and pressed the button on the control panel. Inside the room, a light blinked, which drew Detective Marsh's attention.

"You think about that for a moment, Frank. Think about how they must've felt when you rammed the bottle inside them."

"Detective, please," the lawyer pleaded, but Detective Marsh had already left the room.

***

"You sure about this?" Detective Marsh asked.

Chase nodded.

"Positive. The clinic… all the girls attended the clinic. That's how he's targeting them. What we don't know is how he found out who these patients were. Stitts called the director, and they have no record of Frank ever working there, volunteer or otherwise."

Marsh chewed his lip for a moment.

"Well, how'd you get the list then? It can't be that hard to find out who's in rehab, is it?"

Chase and Stitts exchanged a look.

"That's not important. What's important is the link between the victims."

Detective Marsh pinched the bridge of his nose and closed his eyes. A moment later, he looked up.

"Alright, I'll give it a shot. Not that it matters much, anyway. The DA has already told me that we have enough to move forward. But I still want that bastard to say it; I want him to say out loud what he did to those poor girls."

***

"So, look, we know you did it, Frank. That's no longer the question. What I want to know is why you targeted the girls from the rehab clinic? Have something against ex-users?"

Frank's face, which had remained relatively stoic throughout the interview process, suddenly broke and Marsh smiled.

"Yeah, we know about that, too. Why don't you just come out with it, Frank."

When the man across from him offered no reply, Marsh sighed heavily, laying it on thick now.

"I know it sounds cliched, but it will make you feel better. Look, I've been on this side of the table more times than I care to count. It'll feel—"

Frank raised his head and stared Marsh directly in the eyes.

"I'll only speak to her," he said softly.

Marsh's brow furrowed.

"Who?"

"The FBI Agent. The pretty one with the dark hair. I'll only speak to her."

Chapter 46

"**WHAT DO YOU MEAN** he'll only talk to me?" Chase asked.

Detective Marsh shrugged.

"No idea; I asked him about the clinic and he said he'll only talk to you."

"Yeah, I don't think that's a good idea," Stitts said in a voice that suggested he was speaking to himself.

Chase rightly ignored him.

"Good. Maybe I can get him to open up, maybe—"

Marsh averted his eyes and crossed his arms over his chest.

"I'm with Stitts on this one. I don't think it's a good idea either."

Anger started to build inside her and in her present agitated state, Chase was unsure of how long she could keep it at bay.

"What do you mean? He asked for me and—"

"You're too close," Stitts interjected. "He almost took you."

Chase's lips twisted into a sneer and she felt her cheeks get hot.

"Fuck off, he was never going to 'take me.' He never almost 'took me.' I'm not some—"

Detective Marsh stepped between them.

"Relax," he said, exchanging a look with Stitts.

"Oh, that's how it's going to be, then? A fucking bromance? An all-boys club, is it? You going to tug each—"

"Five minutes," Detective Marsh said. He reached out and gently gripped the outside of her arms. "You've got five minutes. Any more than that, and you could compromise this entire case. Do you understand?"

Chase didn't care for the man's condescending tone and shook herself free.

"Five minutes… I bet I get more out of him in five minutes than you have all fucking day," she muttered under her breath as she made her way to the door.

***

"You can go," Frank told his lawyer as soon as Chase stepped into the room.

The man looked incredulous.

"What? Surely—"

"I said, you can go," Frank repeated.

Chase felt her heart rate increase. It wasn't because she was scared at the prospect of being alone with Frank, but rather because she knew that Detective Marsh and Stitts were looking on and any false step might send them to break this up.

And she needed to *know*.

"I don't think this is—"

Frank, whose eyes had been on Chase ever since she'd entered the room, turned to face his lawyer.

"Leave now, or you're fired."

The man's face twisted into a pretzel, but he scooped up his things and did as he was asked without another word.

Chase waited for the door to close behind them and then stepped forward and leaned on her side of the metal desk.

"What I don't get," she began slowly, "is why you left the condom but wiped your fingerprints. Surely, someone as intelligent as you wouldn't have made a simple mistake such as that, did you?"

"I told you, I didn't do this."

"I'd love to believe you, Frank, I really would. But we've got your DNA at the scene, the victims' clothes were found in your house, and you've already admitted to sleeping with each and every one of them. Really, who else could have done it?"

Frank leveled his eyes at her.

"You're going to get me out of here," he said in a tone that she hadn't heard before.

"Well, if you didn't do it, then you have nothing to fear, do you?" Chase raised a hand in mock salute. "Just put your faith in the justice system of the good ol' U S of A, and ye shall be set free."

"They'll crucify me; any jury who hears about what that bitch Rebecca Hall says I did, and they'll line up to put the electrodes on my scalp."

"Well, lucky for you, the state of Illinois doesn't have the death penalty," she held her hands out. "Ho hum. But if you want me to help you out, you've got to give me something— *anything* I can work with. Let's start with the clinic… why did you target girls from there? Easier still, how did you even know who attended—"

Chase stopped when she realized that Frank was smirking and shaking his head.

"What?" she snapped. She'd come into the room with a clear idea of the narrative she wanted to play out, and this wasn't that. This was a game, and Chase had no patience for games. "What's so funny?"

"You misheard, that's all."

Chase frowned.

"Misheard? What did I mishear?"

Frank lifted his eyes again.

"I said, you're going to get me out of here. *You.*"

Now it was Chase's turn to chuckle.

"And why the hell would I do that, hmm?"

Frank whispered something that she didn't pick up, and she leaned closer to the man.

"What was that? What'd you—"

Frank's hand shot out and he grabbed her left wrist and flipped it over.

"Because I know your secret," he hissed, his breath hot on her ear. "And Craig told me what you did."

Chase gasped and—

Frank was smiling, and he brushed his hair back from his face with one hand. Sweat fell from his knuckles onto Chase's cheek, but she paid it no notice.

The man grunted, and his hips rocked forward.

Chase moaned, and her eyes slowly started to close. Her own fingers were grabbing at his skin—first his triceps, then his back, then his buttocks—her nails raking across his flesh.

Yes! Her mind cried. Yes! Please!

The door to the interview room flew open and Stitts burst through. Frank immediately let go of her wrist and leaned backward. Chase also pulled away, rising to her feet and rubbing at the soft skin just below the ball of her hand.

"Don't you fucking touch her!" Stitts yelled, striding across the room. "Don't you fucking touch her!"

Even when Martinez had beaten Stitts and tied him to the bedpost, Chase had never seen the man this angry.

"Don't you ever—"

Detective Marsh finally stormed into the room and pulled Stitts back.

"Calm down, he just touched her, that's all," then to Chase, the detective said, "You okay?"

Chase nodded and swallowed. Her throat suddenly felt impossibly dry.

"Fine—I'm fine."

Stitts looked at her for a good three seconds without saying anything.

He cares too much, she thought. *He cares too much and he's going to get hurt.*

The lawyer came into the room next and Stitts whipped around to glare at him.

"Keep your fucking client under control!" he snapped.

The man's eyes bulged.

"I—I—I was out of the room. I couldn't... I—I didn't..."

Stitts wrapped an arm around Chase's shoulders and ushered her toward the door. As he did, he leaned close and said, "What did he say to you? What did Frank say to you? It was too soft to pick it up on the audio."

Chase swallowed again before answering.

"Nothing," she replied at last. "He didn't say anything."

Chapter 47

I KNOW YOUR SECRET... Craig told me what you did.

"You're sure he said nothing?" Marsh asked.

Chase rolled her eyes.

"I—"

The door to the observation room suddenly opened, and the three of them, all on edge, whipped around. Chase even thought she saw Stitts's hand slip to the butt of his gun.

They relaxed when they saw that it was only Detective Timmons.

"Bug Eyes has found something on the video footage from the club. Wants you to see it right away," he said.

Chase looked at Stitts.

"Bug Eyes? Who the hell is Bug Eyes?"

"Our computer guy," Marsh informed her with a smirk. "We should check this out."

***

"Watch," the man who called himself Bug Eyes, likely on account of his ridiculously over-sized spectacles, said, as if Stitts, Chase, and Marsh were doing anything but, "*There.*"

The grainy outline of a woman passed across the computer screen. Just when it appeared as if she would exit the frame, she turned and looked at the camera. Bug Eyes hit pause, and Chase leaned forward.

"What? Who is that?"

"This video here is from the night that Bernice Wilson was murdered and this—" The man clicked a few buttons and the monitor split vertically. A second later, another video started that was just like the first: a woman entered the frame and turned to face the camera. " — is from when Leah Morgan was murdered."

Marsh leaned forward and then rocked back.

"Yeah, so? It looks like the same person, but I bet there were a dozen or more people who were at the club on both nights."

"Not a dozen; three. And only one," Bug Eyes opened a folder on his desk and pulled out a photograph, "looks like Rebecca Hall."

Chase gaped.

"What?"

Bug Eyes spun his ergonomic chair around, a smirk plastered on his narrow face.

"I mean, I can't be sure, the footage is like four-eight P or something, but I'm almost positive it's her."

"Naw, I don't think so," Marsh said.

"What? It doesn't *just* look like her, it looks *exactly* like her. That's Rebecca Hall, I'm sure of it," Chase looked over at Stitts for support, but the man appeared to be deliberately averting his gaze.

What's wrong with you, Stitts? Back me up!

"I—I'm not so sure," Marsh said, shaking his head.

"Well, our computer models suggest that it's—"

"Go for a walk, Bug Eyes," Marsh said. "Go on."

Bug Eyes nodded and followed the order.

Then, to Chase's utmost surprise, Stitts also made his way toward the door.

"I'm going to grab a coffee, you want?"

***

I know your secret... Craig told me what you did.

"I asked you before, Chase. What did Frank—"

Chase interrupted Detective Marsh.

"Did you not hear Bug Head or whatever his name is? Rebecca was there, at the club on both—"

"What did Frank say to you, Chase?"

She shook her head.

"This is getting ridiculous. I told both of you, he said, *I didn't do it,* or something like that. That's it. Why would I lie?"

Detective Marsh looked her over.

"And you believe him now?"

"No, not *now.* I've been adamant since the beginning, since arresting Frank, that something was off about this. That—"

Marsh threw up his hands.

"Yeah, and you said the same thing about Jason Portman!"

"And I was right about that, by the way."

"I know people like you, Chase, I meet them every day. The hard truth is that you don't want to catch the killer."

"What?" Chase's ears started to burn, and she turned to face her accuser. "What the *fuck* are you talking about?"

Detective Marsh lowered his eyes.

"It doesn't matter. The DA is—"

"The fuck it doesn't! Tell me what you mean by that, that I don't want to catch this guy."

Chase ground her teeth and tried to stem her anger.

It didn't work.

"You don't really want to catch the killer, the uh, what do you guys call them? The unsubs... yeah, that's it. You don't want to catch the unsub because that brings finality, and for you types, there's always that one killer that got away, the one case that you couldn't solve. And that grinds at you, eats at you like a—"

"You know nothing about me!" Chase shouted. "You don't know fucking—"

Stitts suddenly came through the door, a tray of coffees in his hand.

"Woah! What the hell! I go away for three minutes and you two are either about to fuck or about to fight," he smiled as he said this, but neither Chase nor Marsh returned the gesture. "Well? Which is it?"

"Neither," Marsh said through pursed lips. "It doesn't matter. The DA has approved the charges. Frank will stay here overnight, and then he'll be shuttled for a bail hearing in the morning."

Chase wanted to say more—she also wanted to punch Detective Marsh in the face—but Stitts spoke up first.

"Then I guess our work here is done," he said, extending a hand. "I doubt we were any help, but in the very least I hope we were good company."

"I've had worse, trust me on that," Marsh said. Then he turned to Chase and without pretense, he said, "Agent Adams, it was a pleasure meeting you."

He held his hand out to her, but Chase, who was still shell-shocked, didn't accept it.

"That's it? Seriously? What about the video of Rebecca Hall? What are the odds of her being there? That's not at all suspicious to you guys?"

The expression on Detective Marsh's face, which had been mildly pleasant up until this point, suddenly turned sour.

"Like I said, the DA has approved the—"

"Yeah, I heard—"

Stitts laid a hand on her shoulder.

"Let it go, Chase," he said quietly. "Let it go."

And with that, the two of them started toward the door.

Chapter 48

"SO THAT'S IT THEN?" Chase asked, trying not to pout.

Agents Stitts's grip on the steering wheel tightened, yet he kept his eyes trained on the road ahead.

"The charges have been filed, Chase," Stitts said in his usual calm voice. "There's not much we can do now without undermining Detective Marsh and his whole team. The DA has signed off on it, and there's more than enough evidence for a conviction. Shit, if they got Scott Peterson for the murder of his wife and unborn child on the basis of a single strand of hair, Frank Carruthers is fucked."

Chase mulled this over, three times biting back a scathing remark that she knew would only anger her partner and increase the growing rift between them.

But what about that shit that you said at the Café? Does that not matter? What about what I told you? What about Rebecca Hall being at the club on the days the girls were murdered?

"So, we let them get away with it then," Chase finally said.

Stitts's eyebrows knitted, and he finally turned to look at her.

"Who? Who gets away with it?"

"The person responsible for killing those girls," she said bluntly.

Stitts let out a loud sigh.

"It might be embarrassing to contradict Detective Marsh now," Chase said, "but imagine the outrage when six months from now Frank Carruthers is behind bars and yet more bodies, more girls with their throats slit and genitals mutilated start showing up all around Chicago. Imagine how embarrassing *that* will be."

Stitts turned back to the road.

"Look, Chase, the best we can do is file a report with a recommendation. It's not technically our case, after all; the killer never crossed state lines, there's no element of terror involved, at least not in the new sense of the word, so it's all up to Detective Marsh. We're only here to lend a hand."

"Yeah, where have I heard that before... Stitts, we can make this our case—look, all we have to do is claim that what happened to Rebecca Hall was the first incident leading up to the murders, and that happened in Boston. Then we can have Boston and Chicago, crimes that have clearly taken place in two different states. Give us that, and we could take over the case, and do it right."

Chase observed Stitts closely as she spoke and noticed that the crow's feet at the corners of his eyes grew progressively deeper before eventually relaxing. This was becoming a trend with him, something that Chase had noticed over the last few days: the man tended to squint, a micro gesture, every time he was dealing with some internal turmoil.

"You really think Frank's innocent, don't you?"

"Don't you?" Chase shot back.

Stitts didn't answer her question directly, choosing instead to veer slightly in another direction.

"What is it then? Frank has an accomplice?"

Could it be Craig? But what about his alibi? Was Susan Datcher lying? And Rebecca at the club... what in the hell was that about?

"More like a shadow," Chase blurted, for reasons she didn't really understand. And yet the word seemed to fit, more so than the charges against Frank Carruthers.

When she'd touched Leah Morgan, she'd felt that something was off... she'd felt someone else there, watching.

A shadow.

A shadow suspect.

The word seemed to resonate with Stitts as well, as although he didn't say anything, she noticed that his crow's feet twitched again. They drove in silence for another five minutes and Chase realized with dismay that they were heading back to their hotel room.

"I'm tired," Stitts said, putting an effective end to the conversation. "I need to sleep on this, Chase. I feel the same way you do, although not as strongly. There's something here that doesn't fit, something that just isn't right."

Chase nodded. Her partner's response was the best she could hope for in this situation. She too was tired, but she was also paradoxically wired. It had been so long since her last fix that Chase felt jumpy, twitchy, like someone who was amped up on a case of Mountain Dew and hadn't slept for three days. A recipe for bad decisions. She knew that a crash was inevitable; this had happened to her once before, back when she was with Tyler Tisdale. They had gone three days without a fix, and for the first half of it, Chase felt okay. And this had given her a sense of hope, hope that while she felt the aftereffects of her heroin use—the trembling, the nervousness, the sensitivity to light and sound—she didn't really feel like she *had* to use. But by the fifth day, everything changed.

Chase started vomiting, and when she wasn't purging her guts, all she wanted to do was to sleep. She slept for as long as she could, hoping that when she woke up this would all be gone. Only she could never get more than twenty minutes at a time before her body snapped alert, her eyes searching, her fingertips feeling for her next fix.

When they arrived at the hotel room a half hour later, the idea of a shadow had taken hold. A shadow suspect, one that can only be seen in the presence of the person making it; the presence of Frank Carruthers.

And the only way to catch the shadow, to catch the real unknown subject responsible for the murders of Bernice Wilson, Meg Docker, Kirsty Buchanan, and Leah Morgan, was to re-create their final moments.

Chase knew this the way that she knew she was a heroin addict through and through.

Chapter 49

CHASE STARED AT THE shadows on the ceiling that first elongated before melting into the darkness entirely. Stitts was lying in a bed not five feet from her, snoring softly. He had packed it in early, on account of their flight, which was scheduled to leave at the crack of dawn.

Over a shared scotch from the minibar, Chase tried to convince Stitts to change his mind, to tell Marsh to hold off with arraigning Frank so that they could do a little more digging.

There were so many things that just didn't make sense, so many pieces to the puzzle that were missing.

At first, Stitts had been implacable, but over time he seemed to soften somewhat. That all changed, however, when Director Hampton called Stitts's cell phone and told him that their tickets were booked, and that they were due back in Quantico for a briefing on another case in the morning.

Although it hadn't been explicitly stated, it was obvious that Detective Marsh had preemptively called Hampton to offer his thanks for the FBI's involvement. And, of course, to ensure that Stitts didn't change his mind and start poking around a case the man had already concluded was closed.

Chase closed her eyes and tried to push thoughts of the shadow suspect from her mind. Part of her wanted to be on board, to be part of the team, the way that Agent Stitts seemed to be even though he'd expressed his concerns about the loose ends as well. Hell, she wanted their killer to be Frank Carruthers.

A car pulled into the hotel parking lot, awakening the shadows on the ceiling. Like fluffy clouds in a blue sky, they started to form a face before Chase's eyes: the face of the man wearing aviator sunglasses.

Is this going to happen to you, Georgina? Eventually, is everyone going to just forget about you, take your file and put it on a dusty pile in some shitty basement marked Cold Cases? Has that already happened?

Chase swallowed hard.

Somewhere out there was the man who had taken her sister from her all those years ago. And nobody cared.

Except for Chase.

And somewhere out there was the unsub responsible for the deaths—the brutal slayings and mutilation—of four beautiful women.

With a deep breath, Chase pulled back her bed sheet. Her body was slick with sweat, and her hands were shaking as she first put on the outfit she'd worn to the club, and then slipped her jeans and blouse on top.

Stitts was trusting as well as caring; his car keys were on the table just as they'd been the last time she'd taken them. As she picked them up and made her way to the door, she turned back to look at her partner. She knew that the man had gone out on a limb for her, probably on more than one occasion, and she felt bad about what she was about to do.

But she felt worse about what had happened to Leah, Meg, Bernice, and Kirsty.

And Georgina.

That was the worst of all because she'd been there. Because she was responsible.

"I'm sorry, Stitts," Chase said softly. "But I'm not like you; I can't just let this go."

Others may have forgotten about her sister, but Chase never would.

***

"We've gotta move him," Chase said, leveling her eyes at the police officer standing in front of her. "We've gotta move him now."

The officer had a blank stare on his face, and for a brief moment, Chase thought that for the second time in as many nights, the man didn't recognize her. She debated pulling out and flashing her FBI badge but thought that might be overdoing it. The man *had* to know who she was, given the way that Detective Marsh had chastised him at their meeting.

He's just confused, she thought.

"I think I should call Detective Marsh, let him know what's going on," Officer Stevenson said.

Chase shook her head.

"I'm under strict orders from FBI Director Hampton to move Frank Carruthers to a secure location. Tonight. Now."

The man was shaking his head even before Chase stopped speaking, and she knew that she was losing him.

"I'm a goddamn FBI Agent, Stevenson, and you know that stunt you pulled the other day? Calling me sweetie? Telling me to, *move along, pretty lady*? You want me to make that public knowledge? You look like a guy who wants to make detective one day," Chase stared at him intently. "No, not detective... Chief, maybe? Well, I'll tell you what, pal, with all this *#metoo* bullshit going on these days, one complaint about a sexist comment and next week you'll be handing out parking tickets."

The man's frown became a scowl, and Chase wondered if she had taken it too far.

"Sexist comment?" he said. "I didn't—"

Chase softened her tone.

"Look, Officer Stevenson, this is my first case. Seriously, I'm straight out of the Academy—literally came straight from Quantico—and when FBI Director Hampton told me to come get Frank Carruthers I was skeptical, too. But he's my boss. Shit, he might be technically your boss, too. And now it's almost midnight, and you want to wake Detective Marsh? I'll tell you what, there's no way that I'd second-guess a superior's orders and wake my boss up in the middle of the night. No way, no how."

The man's face contorted. He looked constipated.

"I don't know," Stevenson said, glancing over his shoulder at Frank Carruthers, who was sleeping in his cell. "Is there some sort of paperwork, at least?"

A hint of a smile formed on Chase's lips as she reached into her coat pocket and pulled out a folded sheet of paper. She handed it to the man and he started to open it, but before he did, Chase reached out and put her hand on top of his.

"If it makes you feel any better, you can come with us. As an escort. It'll look great on your record, helping out the FBI on a high-profile case such as this one. But we have to be quick."

As predicted, the man's eyebrows rose up his forehead. Stevenson *was* young, maybe twenty-five, and had probably seen too many movies and expected to be hanging out an open window with his gun drawn.

Let him think that, Chase mused. *Let him think whatever he wants so long as it gets Frank out of that cell. Let testosterone drive his actions.*

"There's seriously a death threat on his life? Here? In Chicago?" Stevenson asked, tapping the folded piece of paper on an open palm.

Chase nodded.

"You'd be surprised at how many times this happens. In fact, I'd be willing to bet that death threats against the accused in cases that involve women and children happen more often than not. Most of the time they're bogus, but this is a risk that the FBI isn't willing to take." An image of Agent Chris Martinez's face an instant before Stitts blew the back of his brains out flashed in her mind and Chase shuddered. "Especially after what happened last time. Anyways, we're just moving him to a safe location, to make sure that he can get to his arraignment tomorrow morning. At the courthouse, we'll have additional security. And then that bastard will hang for what he did to those women."

She could almost see the gears inside Officer Stevenson's head turning. They were rusty gears, but once they got going, things slowly fell into place.

"All right," the man said at last, "but I'm coming with you. And as soon as we get to the secure location, I'm calling Detective Marsh. I don't care what time it is."

Chase couldn't help the smile that formed on her lips.

Yeah, you do that.

Chapter 50

"YOU WANNA TAKE THE squad car? Lights flashing?" Officer Stevenson asked.

"I told you you'd get me out of here," a sleepy Frank Carruthers said under his breath.

"Shut up," Chase hissed, tugging on the links between the handcuffs. Then to Stevenson, she said, "No, we need to keep this under the radar."

The police officer nodded, while Frank squirmed.

"Be quiet," Chase whispered. "Just be quiet."

They made it to the front desk without incident, which was manned by the same woman who had let Chase in earlier in the day.

"Paul?" the woman asked as they approached. "What's going on here?"

Officer Stevenson cleared his throat.

"The FBI has received death threats against Frank Carruthers. Agent Adams and I are going to escort him to a secure location."

Chase had to fight back a smile. Things were working out better than she could've expected; this narrative was much more convincing coming from the officer who the woman at the desk knew on a first name basis rather than from her, even given her credentials.

"Does Detective Marsh know?" the woman asked.

Stevenson looked over at Chase and, for a split second, she thought he was going to break and revert to his initial instinct to call his boss before they did anything.

"He'll be informed by the Director of the FBI in the morning. It's imperative that we get this prisoner out of the building as soon as possible."

The woman's eyes widened.

"Am I in danger? Should we evacuate the building?"

Chase shook her head.

"It's just a precaution."

"A death threat?" Frank asked. Chase pulled down on the handcuffs, straining the man's shoulders to make him shut up. "The cuffs... they're too tight."

"I've got the, uh, *transfer* papers right here," Officer Stevenson said as he held out the folded piece of paper that Chase had given to him outside Frank's cell.

Chase pulled down on Frank's cuffs again, and he cried out, drawing everyone's attention.

"Got the keys?" she asked, still leaning on the man's wrists. "I'll loosen these just a bit."

Stevenson took one look at the anguish on Frank's face, and then reached onto his belt and handed Chase a set of handcuff keys.

"We should go," Chase said quickly. Officer Stevenson nodded and handed the sheet of paper over to the woman behind the desk. She looked up, and Chase offered her a smile. "Thanks."

And with that, Chase hurried toward the door, shoving Frank into the night. She didn't wait for Officer Stevenson, but she knew that he was right behind her.

Chase was barely outside before she heard the secretary shout.

"Officer Stevenson! Paul!"

Frank tried to turn to see what was going on, but Chase pushed him forward. Then Chase broke into a light jog, moving as quickly as she could without risking a fall. If they went down, the gig would be up.

"Paul! *Paul!*"

Officer Stevenson turned to Chase and said, "Hey, wait up just a sec. Slow down."

But Chase didn't wait up or slow down; if anything, she sped out.

She overheard shouts about the paper being blank, that they needed to provide a proper release form, even if there was a threat to Frank's life.

Chase ignored all of this and opened the back door of Stitts's rental.

"What the hell is going on? Where are you taking me?" Frank demanded.

Chase shoved the man inside, slamming the door closed behind him. As she moved to the driver's door, she realized that Stevenson was sprinting toward her, holding up the unfolded blank sheet of paper that she'd given him.

His face was twisted into a mask of confusion and anger.

"I'm sorry," Chase said as she slid behind the wheel.

Agent Stitts's Taurus had already disappeared into the night even before Officer Stevenson made it to his car.

Chapter 51

"**WHERE ARE YOU TAKING** me?" Frank asked from the backseat.

Chase didn't answer right away. Her eyes kept snapping up to the mirror to see if Officer Stevenson was after them, if his police cherries were lighting up the night sky.

To this point, however, there was no sign of him. But it would be foolish to think that it wasn't just a matter of time.

"What the hell is going on? Where are you taking me?"

Again, Chase ignored the man. Even though she and Agent Stitts had gone to the area several times, this was her first time behind the wheel, and she made several wrong turns before getting back to something she recognized. In the end, this probably served her well, as her erratic driving might have thrown Stevenson for a loop.

Either way, Chase knew it couldn't be long before every cop in the city, and Agent Stitts, came for her.

"Listen, lady," Frank pleaded, his voice trembling now. "I was just being an ass before, I don't know anything about you. No secrets or anything. Just let me go. Shit, take me back to the station if you have to."

Chase didn't say anything, she just leaned over the steering wheel and followed the brilliant lights that made up the words 'Club 101.' Finding parking was next to impossible at this time of night—coming on two a.m.—but that didn't matter; she wasn't worried about getting a ticket.

Chase double-parked and then jumped out of the car. She opened the rear door and stared at Frank.

"Turn around," she ordered. Chase had cataloged everything that the man had done since she'd taken him from his cell, everything that he'd said, every blink, every breath, every twitch. If she had had any doubt of the man's innocence, this final look sealed it: he was scared of her. And a man who had already slit four women's throats wouldn't be scared in Chase's presence.

He would be excited.

Frank, eyes wide, shifted his hips so that his hands were behind him. Chase reached into her pocket and withdrew the handcuff keys that Officer Stevenson had given her and was about to unlock Frank's handcuffs when she hesitated.

Her fingers were shaking so badly that she could barely fit the key in the lock.

What am I doing? What in God's name am I doing?

Chase had broken perhaps a dozen laws already and would break at least twice that number before the night was out.

Part of her wanted to slide the keys back into her pocket, get back into the car and drive to the police station and drop Frank off. If she did that, then maybe — *maybe* — she wouldn't be arrested.

But if she went through with her plan tonight, not only was there zero chance she would ever be an FBI agent again, but Chase would most likely find herself behind bars. And that meant that Georgina would be lost forever.

Chase shook her head.

What was the old adage? It is better for ten guilty people to be set free than to incarcerate one innocent person… something like that, anyway.

This was the final piece, the tipping point. There was no going back now.

With a deep breath, Chase removed Frank's cuffs and the man immediately started to massage his wrists.

He turned to her then, and for the briefest moment, sheer fury flashed over his handsome features. Chase's heart palpitated, and she thought that perhaps he had tricked her.

That she had been wrong all this time, and that she was about to become his fifth victim.

But then his face softened.

"Are you going to tell me what the hell we're doing here?" Chase helped him out of the vehicle.

"Tell me just one thing," Chase said quickly. "Those two other girls… Gwen and Tiffany… how did you get to their house after the bar?"

Frank's brow lowered.

"I don't know, I can't remember."

Chase grabbed his arm and squeezed.

"Think, goddammit. *Think.*"

Frank grit his teeth.

"We drove… yeah, I took an Uber to Gwen's house and Tiffany drove us."

Chase nodded.

"That's what I thought," she said, letting go of him.

"Now, are you going to tell me what we're doing here?" Chase looked up at the bright lights as she spoke.

"We're going to reenact what happened with Leah, Meg, Bernice, and Kirsty. We're going to try to bring a shadow out of the woodworks."

Frank's face screwed up.

"Shadow? Look, lady, you're fucking high or something. I don't know what Craig said to you, or what you think—"

Chase shut him up by roughly guiding him towards Club 101.

As they walked, Chase considered the very real possibility that Frank might run off. That when they separated, when she was alone in the club and Frank was outside, that he might just bolt.

But Chase didn't think so. Even though Frank hadn't killed the girls, he was at least partly responsible for their deaths. If it hadn't been for him, if he hadn't picked them up outside the club, they'd likely still be alive today.

Besides, she had no choice; it was a risk she was going to have to take.

"We're going to catch the bastard that did this to those girls, and you're going to help me."

Frank glared at her for a moment, but eventually, he lowered his eyes.

Then he nodded.

It appeared as if both of them wanted to make amends and to stop a serial killer.

Chapter 52

CHASE HAD ONE DRINK inside the club and then headed outside much like she had the other day, her focus on the shawarma shop.

She ordered the same thing—a loaded shish taouk—but the thought of eating anything right now made her stomach curdle.

And then she waited, trying not to get lost in the crowd. She'd tossed her jeans and sweatshirt into Stitts's car, and now, wearing only her short dress, the breeze threatened to lift the hem and expose the gun and holster she'd hastily reconfigured to fit on her thigh.

A minute passed, then two. When Chase had been staring at the soggy wrap for more than five minutes, she lowered her head. After everything that she'd done tonight, everything that had gone surprisingly right, the biggest piece had failed.

Frank had run.

And now Chase figured it might be best if she did the same. Just get the fuck out of Chicago, drive somewhere, find a rack of heroin, and just—

"Hi there, you having a good night?"

Chase whipped around so fast that she nearly dropped her shish taouk. Frank was standing there, one eyebrow raised, his lips twisted into a smirk.

The man exuded so much charm that even in this manufactured scenario, the scenario that she had come up with, Chase was almost taken in by him.

Why did he have to prey on recovering addicts? He could get any woman he wanted.

"The night's going just fine, thank you."

"Fine? Just fine?" Frank looked up at the clear sky, the people around him. "It's a beautiful night and you're a beautiful woman, your night shouldn't just be fine. It should be better than fine. It should be *amazing*."

For some reason, Chase found herself blushing.

"I wouldn't mind amazing," she said softly, averting her eyes.

"Well, I don't know about *amazing*, but I bet I can get you at least halfway there. You're gonna have to do the rest."

***

They couldn't go back to Frank's house, of course; it was still being combed for evidence. And they couldn't go back to the hotel, even though it was highly unlikely that Stitts would be there—at this point, there was no doubt in her mind that he was out looking for her and Frank—it was just too far; all the victims had lived within walking distance of the club.

There was only one place she knew that would be unlocked and close enough to get to on foot, and while it was risky, Chase was running out of options.

I should've thought this through more, she mused. But then again, if Chase had thought her plan through completely, she wouldn't have been in this scenario in the first place. *We'll go there and hope the shadow follows—we've only got one shot at this.*

As they walked down the street, hand-in-hand, Chase let her mind wander. Normally this was a dangerous game, but in this situation, Chase wanted to recreate the scenario as accurately as possible. She thought back to when she'd arrived in Leah Morgan's apartment and had first approached the woman's blood-soaked mattress. Then she imagined touching her arm, her cold, dead skin, ever so slightly.

A flash of Frank's sweaty face, the muscles in his shoulders and chest tensing with every thrust, filled her mind.

Yes, that's it… I like that… I like that.

"My place is this way," she said softly, guiding Frank down a side street. The man offered her a confused look but didn't resist.

He was all in now. Frank was the charming one, but Chase had managed to suck him into her game.

When Chase had visited Leah Morgan's apartment, what felt like a month ago, she had noticed that the neighbors' door had been ajar, and she could pick up the distinct scent of fresh paint coming from within. She'd peeked inside and seen a fridge and maybe a couch. And later, Marsh had confirmed that the neighbors were out at the time of Leah's murder, that they were living somewhere else while the minor renovations took place.

That's where we'll go.

It took ten minutes, even walking slowly, during which time they exchanged no words. When they got to the apartment, however, Frank stopped and reached for her.

"Here?" he asked, his eyes wide. Even though he hadn't killed Leah, he had been in her apartment that night.

And he'd seen the crime scene photos.

"Yeah, I'm just up here," Chase said with a look.

Frank hesitated, and she could see him struggling to swallow.

"What's wrong? You don't want to come up?"

With a strong tug, she managed to move him toward the door. Before he could resist, she pushed the door open and yanked him over the threshold.

"This is—"

Chase tilted her chin upward and kissed Frank full on the lips.

The gesture took him so completely by surprise that he stumbled backward. A good seven inches taller than she, Chase had to get on her tippy-toes to grab the back of his head and pull him into the kiss and to prevent them both from toppling.

It took a few seconds, but Frank eventually started to kiss her back. When his arms started to wrap around her, Chase pulled away and playfully shoved his chest.

"Not until we get upstairs," she said.

Chase led the way, but the closer they got to Leah's apartment, which was still covered in yellow tape, the more slowly Frank moved. By the time they reached the landing, she was practically dragging him.

But when she turned right instead of left, he started to move a little more freely. The apartment door across from Leah's wasn't even locked; with all the commotion and police activity, the painters must have forgotten.

They stepped inside together, and Chase closed the door gently behind them.

For a moment, neither of them spoke.

And then a scared looking Frank closed his eyes and said, "What now? What the hell do we do now?"

Chapter 53

"I'M NOT A BAD guy," Frank said. He stared at his hands as he spoke, an indication that he was being genuine. "I didn't want anything bad to happen to those girls. I had no idea."

Chase adjusted her dress and tried to make herself comfortable on the edge of the bed. They hadn't been inside the apartment for more than five minutes before Frank started to open up. Chase had taken Stitts's approach, and it had worked like a charm. She had remained silent and let Frank get uncomfortable to the point of *needing* to fill the dead air.

And she got the impression that once Frank started, he would be unable to stop. A man like this... he didn't strike Chase as the type who got the opportunity to be vulnerable very often.

"And I think with Rebecca... I swear to God, I did nothing to her. She was fucking crazy, and I left her—that's it. She's batshit crazy. I kinda feel bad for her; I mean, she has issues, but I had to get out of there. It was just toxic, man. The relationship was fucking toxic, and I couldn't stick around anymore."

Chase watched as the man's face sagged and his eyes became moist with tears.

She tried to put herself in his shoes for a moment. Tried to imagine being arrested for four murders he didn't commit, of having his life flipped upside down. Frank Carruthers was no gentleman, of that Chase was certain; but he wasn't a murderer, either. Chase thought briefly of some of the men she'd been with in the past, about the things she'd done to get her fix, how she'd used them, and realized that Frank wasn't all that different from her.

"But why the clinic, Frank? How does that fit into this?" she asked softly.

Frank cracked his knuckles and the muscles in his jaw clenched.

"After I moved out here, after the whole Rebecca thing, I just wanted to get laid. I thought it would be easy, especially with the club scene so close, but it wasn't, not really. I'm usually only in town for the weekend, and work tires me out. Sometimes I'm only in town for one day. And these girls, man, they were just so much work."

Chase watched as Frank continuously interlaced and then teased apart his fingers.

"It started by accident, really. I have this friend — Craig — who you met. Well, one day, Craig snapped a picture of a super-hot girl at the clinic and sent it to me. That night, I shit you not, I ran into her outside the bar. She was... ah, fuck, I know this makes me sound like a total asshole, but the truth is this girl was *vulnerable*. And yet, she strangely lacked the baggage of the other chicks that I'd met in town. She wasn't stuck up, wasn't looking for a sugar daddy, to be wined and dined. All she wanted was to feel something, I guess. Anyways, the next week, Craig sent me another pic. Soon, I just skipped the bar altogether. Craig would snap a pic of the new girls at Palisades and he'd chat 'em up, see when they were going out. Then I'd meet them outside and... well..." Frank let his sentence trail off.

A tear fell down his cheek then and, without thinking, Chase reached up and wiped it away.

"I'm so, so sorry about what happened to those girls," Frank said, his voice barely a whisper now. "And I feel so fucking dirty for taking advantage of them, but — "

What happened next surprised even Chase. She reached out and grabbed Frank's hands in hers. The man glanced down at her, a startled expression on his face, and as he did Chase leaned in and kissed him full on the lips. Only it wasn't a stage kiss like they'd shared at the door.

This was real.

Frank's lips were salty with his own tears, and at first, he was reluctant.

But Chase persisted.

She let go of his hands and cuffed the back of his neck, pulling them together. Her tongue found his, and Frank started to kiss her back.

And then his hands were on her shoulders, and then her breasts, gently cupping their round shape, squeezing them, caressing them.

Chase was transported into another world, one in which she was on her back as Frank thrust into her over and over again, driving her ever closer to orgasm. A moan escaped her lips, and she was about to reach for Frank's jeans when he suddenly pulled away.

Chase opened her eyes and stared at Frank.

"I can't," he said quietly, squeezing his forehead. "This is fucked-up—I can't. I *can't*. Not after what happened to the others."

Chase was confused; she wasn't sure what she'd imagined and what had really happened.

"You can, Frank. I'm not one of those girls, I'm not—"

Frank's dark eyes darted to the scars on the inside of her left forearm, the ones that in her haste she had forgotten to cover with makeup.

And then it wasn't just Frank who was crying, but Chase was crying along with him.

"I'm sorry," she said, her voice hitching. "I'm sorry. I just want to find her. To find my sister."

Through blurred vision, she saw Frank look at her, not with pity as some might have, but with shame.

"Go," she told him, hiding her face. "Get out of here before they come for you."

Frank's jaw clenched again, and, for a moment, it looked like he might stay, like he might sit beside her on the edge of the bed and hold her.

Oh, how she wanted to be held.

"Go!" Chase shouted, and Frank bolted from the apartment, once again leaving her alone with her thoughts.

Chapter 54

"SO, YOU WANT TO fuck?" The man with the aviator sunglasses asked, a shit-eating grin on his face. "I'll tell you what, after we fuck, you can have some of this."

The man pulled a comically large syringe from somewhere beneath the soiled bed sheet and held it up for Chase to see. She reached for it, but to her horror, she realized that she had no hands: her forearms ended in stumps— in burnt, mangled stumps.

Chase wanted to scream, but then the man began wagging the syringe and this became the sole focus of her attention.

"Gimme," Chase begged in a childish voice that she barely recognized. "Gimme, gimme, gimme."

"Nuh-uh-ah," the man said, moving the syringe back and forth in a hypnotic motion. "If you want to get high, you're going to have to fuck me."

Chase suddenly felt sick to her stomach, but no matter how hard she tried, she couldn't move away; not only were her hands missing, but her feet had been lopped off as well.

The man in the sunglasses pouted.

"What? You don't want to fuck me?" he asked with a chuckle. "Why not? Your sister sure didn't mind it."

As he spoke, the man pulled back the dirty sheet from under which he had retrieved the syringe, and there, for the first time in over two decades, Chase saw her baby sister.

Georgina's body was blue and bloated and her once vibrant orange hair had been reduced to a greasy, grimy brown.

Chase shut her eyes, but the image of her sister's corpse remained.

"You sure you don't want to get in? It's awfully hot out there."

She shook her head.

"No, no, I'm not getting in there. No matter what, I'm not getting in there, and neither is she."

Chase's eyes snapped open and she stared at her younger sister, who was smiling up at her with swollen, purple lips. She tried to pick Georgina up, to hold her tight, to squeeze her, to never let her go again, but without hands, she just clumsily batted the corpse from side-to-side.

And then the man started to laugh.

It started as a chuckle originating in his throat, but it soon became a full-bodied bellow. A few moments after that, the man's massive body was quaking, his round, bare belly quivering out the sides of his soiled blue overalls.

And then the man's laughter stopped as abruptly as it had started.

"I'm going to save you the trouble," he said in a strange, high-pitch voice, "I'm going to end it right here. I'm going to do to you what he did to me. I'm going to—"

Chapter 55

"—BREAK YOU THE WAY Frank broke me."

Chase awoke disoriented, confused as to where she was. When she realized she was lying in Leah's neighbor's bed, she scolded herself for having fallen asleep.

How could I fall asleep? With everything going on... how is that even possible?

Chase tried to sit up but felt dizzy and lay back down.

There was something wrong with her eyes—her vision was blurred, and the only thing she could make out was a shadow hovering over her.

She tried to speak but managed only a muffled cry.

There was a piece of tape covering her mouth, she realized. Panic set in, panic and confusion, as Chase couldn't be sure if what was happening, what she was feeling, was real or just another vision. But when a hand came down and roughly gripped her wrist, she opted for the former.

He's here... the killer is here and he's on top of me.

But instead of panicking, relief washed over her. Chase was relieved that she was right, that she was going to catch the person responsible for the girls' deaths.

A thought occurred to her then; the other girls hadn't been tied down because they'd been too drunk to struggle.

Chase wasn't tied down, either, but she wasn't drunk. She might have looked wasted, curled up the way she'd been, perhaps mumbling in her sleep, but she was stone-cold sober.

For once.

She was about to toss the bastard off of her and spring to her feet, grabbing for the pistol that she'd hidden under the bed when something caught her eye. Even with blurred vision and in the poor lighting, she saw something plastic clutched in her assailant's free hand.

Something plastic with a silver end that reflected what little light emanated from the hallway.

It was a syringe, Chase realized.

Her breath caught in her throat.

"Oh, now you see it, don't you? And you want it... I know you want it."

Chase tried to squint, to focus her vision, because something wasn't right here; the words... they sounded like they were spoken by a woman. But she couldn't; Chase couldn't even blink. Her eyelids had been propped open. She had no idea when the matchsticks had been put in place, or how it was possible that she hadn't woken up during the process.

I can still flip him off, I can still get out of here. I can still make him pay.

Chase turned her head to one side, and her entire body seemed to turn to liquid.

The reason why she couldn't sit up was that even though the syringe that her assailant held in one hand was half-full, it was evident that just a few minutes ago it had been completely full.

She was high. The bastard had already injected her.

Forgetting that her mouth was taped, Chase tried to speak again, but only managed incoherent mumbles.

"Your mouth is taped because no matter what you say, they won't listen. Your eyes are open because even though you'll see everything that I do to you, it won't matter. They'll all ignore you. I tried... I tried to tell people what Frank did to me, how he played me, got me drunk at that bar, The Farm, how he took advantage of the fact that I was addicted to drugs. And he just comes off as a savior, promising me that he would make it so that I don't need the drugs anymore, that all I need is him."

Chase tried to sit up again, taking her free hand and driving it into the mattress. She managed to shift onto her side, almost making it to a seated position, before she saw the glint of a knife.

"Ah, ah, ah," the woman, for now Chase was sure it was a woman, teased. "Don't even think about it. You handled your dose better than the others, normally they just lie there with their eyes rolling around. But not you. It doesn't matter, there's more where that came from. And you want it, don't you?"

Chase's eyes were so dry at this point that they actually started to water, and she tried with all her might to clench her forehead, to break the matchsticks or dislodge them, but all she accomplished was to strain her muscles.

Chase had no idea how things had gone from her kissing Frank Carruthers on this very bed to now staring death in the face.

And in this case, death came in the form of a woman: in the form of Rebecca Hall.

"Just give up. There's no shame in giving up. One injection, and all your worries will go away."

Chase was staring up at the woman who had murdered Leah, Bernice, Meg, and Kirsty, and yet she found her thoughts preoccupied with Tyler Tisdale and how similar Rebecca's words were to his.

And also how true they were.

Chase knew that if she just allowed Rebecca to inject her with the full dose of heroin, her problems *would* go away. And then it wouldn't matter if her throat was slit, if Georgina was still out there somewhere, if Stitts lost his job.

Nothing would matter.

And a large part of Chase wanted just that.

"You sure you girls don't want a ride? It's awfully hot out there."

Rebecca shifted her weight so that her entire body was pushing down on Chase's left wrist. She was smiling, and Chase realized that she was pretty. Even in the dim lighting and with her blurred vision, she could tell that the woman had pale features, pretty features, and dark hair that swirled about her head.

Chase had been right all along; the victims were selected based on what Frank liked. And when he was done with them, the way he had finished with Rebecca, she would come in and finish the job.

Chase tried to speak again but couldn't even manage a mumble this time.

Rebecca threw her head back and laughed, but there was no humor in the sound.

"You think I'm going to take this off so that you can scream? Beg to be saved?" She held up the syringe and flicked the plunger with her thumb. "This is the only thing that can save you now."

Chase shook her head side to side and as she did she felt one of the matchsticks start to move a little. Not enough so that she could close her eyes, but a little.

Chase didn't want any of those things.

She only had one question.

Maybe it was her desperation, or something else, Chase didn't know. But for some reason, Rebecca reached for and pinched the corner of the tape on her cheek.

"If you scream, I'm going to make you hurt."

Chase nodded and then winced as the tape was pulled back. Her lips felt as if they were being peeled off her face. When the tape was just past the midpoint of her mouth, Chase gasped and inhaled sharply.

"Make it quick, or I'll make it slow," Rebecca said.

Even though her world was spinning, Chase managed to collect herself enough so that she could ask her question.

"Did he do it? Did Frank rape you with a bottle?"

Chapter 56

REBECCA LAUGHED. BEFORE ANSWERING, she roughly
shoved the tape back over Chase's lips. Chase tried to resist by
shaking her head but stopped when her entire world started
to blur and smudge like a TV screen smeared with Vaseline.

"Did he do it? Did Frank do it? Frank did everything to me.
He lied to me, he took advantage of me, he—"

Rebecca suddenly squinted, and she shifted so that her
knee drove painfully into Chase's bicep, forcing her back
down.

"Wait—how do you know about the bottle?" she
demanded.

Chase couldn't answer even if she wanted to; the tape was
covering her mouth again.

"Who are you? Who the fuck are you?"

Rebecca was becoming more agitated with every question
that Chase didn't—couldn't—answer, and she leaned back as
if rearing up to strike.

Chase seized the moment.

She might have been exhausted, she might have been high,
but she was well-trained and in good shape.

Chase rolled away from the pressure on her arm, spinning
onto all fours. She caught Rebecca by surprise and the woman
fell backward off the bed, sending the syringe flying. Chase
swiped the matchsticks away from her eyes and then sighed
as her eyelids closed with a sound reminiscent of wax paper
sliding over tree bark. After blinking rapidly for several
seconds, her vision finally started to clear. And then, without
bothering to remove the tape from her mouth, Chase pounced
on Rebecca who reacted by holding the knife up in front of
her. The blade, which looked like a common steak knife, slid

into Chase's right bicep. She cried out and pulled her arm back, which only served to make a four-inch-long gash through the muscle.

Then Chase threw a punch. She was aiming for Rebecca's chin, but the woman was already moving out of the way of the stream of blood that spilled from Chase's arm, and her fist struck her in the shoulder instead. She retaliated by flailing with the knife, and Chase barely leaned back far enough to avoid being cut again.

Rebecca was snarling like a feral dog as she slashed at the air. Yet her moves were sloppy, uncoordinated; she was only used to attacking women who were so high that they couldn't move.

There was another sound in the room, a strained huffing noise, and it took Chase a moment to realize that was her own breathing coming from behind the duct tape. She reached for the corner and pulled it free, crying out as she did.

Rebecca, who had somehow made her way to a seated position, was now scrambling onto all fours. Chase timed it so that when the woman thrust the knife behind her, she pounced. With both hands, Chase grabbed Rebecca's wrist and gripped it so tightly that she could barely move the knife.

And then Chase threw all of her weight against Rebecca's back, pinning her to the floor. She slammed Rebecca's wrist repeatedly on the parquet tiles until her fingers were bloodied and she had no choice but to let go of the knife. Chase released her hold and lunged for the blade, but before she could grab it, she heard a strange noise.

It sounded hollow, but before she could figure out what it was, something hard cracked against the back of her skull.

Chase collapsed onto her stomach, barely managing to get her hands out in front of her before her face smashed against the floor.

She saw stars, a vast universe of stars embedded in a black chasm.

Moaning, Chase managed to roll over. Rebecca was on her in an instant, sitting on her stomach, her hands encircling her throat.

"I don't know who you are, you fucking bitch, but you're going to die just like the rest of them," Rebecca hissed.

Chase tried to call out, to tell this woman that she was with the FBI, but even if she had managed, it wouldn't have made a difference. Rebecca was beyond reproach, blinded by fury and scorn.

Chase didn't know what Frank had done to her, if he had actually violated her with the bottle, if he'd raped her, but in that moment, it didn't matter; it didn't matter, because this was what Rebecca thought that Frank had done to her.

And it overwhelmed her.

Chase wondered what she would do if she ever met the man in the aviator sunglasses, who must have been well into his fifties or even sixties by now. If she would be able to resist the urge to kill him right there without a second thought.

Chase could feel her esophagus being compressed beneath Rebecca's fingers and tasted blood in her mouth.

Her vision started to narrow again, but this time, she didn't see the universe; she saw an endless black pit.

"Please," she tried to croak, but the only thing that came out of her mouth was a wheeze.

"Why should I listen to you?" Rebecca snapped. "Nobody listened to me when I told them that I was raped. Nobody gave a shit about me, about what I had to say."

As if fueled by the anger of her own words, Rebecca leaned forward and pushed down with all her might on Chase's throat.

Chase started to lose consciousness, lose the sensation of the floor beneath her back, of the blood that trickled down her wounded bicep. She thought briefly about the gun under the bed and somehow managed to lower her eyes to look at it. It was still there, as was the cell phone that she intended to turn on and call Stitts with when she'd caught the killer.

The *real* killer.

This is it, this is how it ends. I'm sorry, Georgina. I'm sorry, Brad. I'm sorry, Felix.

Chase briefly pictured her own funeral, her bawling son and husband staring at the black casket as it was lowered into the earth. And then she thought, strangely, incoherently, that they had a hell of a wake for her, that Brad drank his face off, and what little friends she had laughed at the good times.

She had given them all so much pain while she was alive, that Chase hoped in death she could finally give them some pleasure.

Chapter 57

"I'M STILL OUT HERE, Chase. I'm still out here, waiting for you to save me. It's been more than twenty years, but I never forgot about you. Seeing your face in my mind is the only way I manage to get through every day. Don't give up on me yet, Chase. Don't give up on me, because I haven't given up on you."

Chapter 58

CHASE HEARD A GRUNT and her first thought was that it was her who had made the sound. But when she heard a second grunt and the pressure in her throat suddenly alleviated, she knew that this wasn't the case.

A third grunt, this one preceded by a hollow thud, and Rebecca's hands fell away completely.

Chase's back arched, and she coughed violently. Bright white flashes spread across her vision as she barked, trying desperately to fill her lungs that burned as if she had inhaled mustard gas.

She blinked rapidly and managed to roll away from Rebecca who had collapsed beside her. Chase scrambled to her knees and looked around, wondering what the hell had happened, why had Rebecca stopped strangling her.

And then she saw a male figure standing over both of them, looking down at their bruised and battered bodies. Her vision was still clouded, and for an instant, she thought that he was wearing overalls, faded blue overalls, with a bare chest jutting from the top.

Chase coughed again, and finally managed to draw a full breath. As she did, her vision finally cleared completely.

It wasn't the man from the van, of course, it was someone else.

"Agent Stitts?"

The man didn't answer and instead bent down to pick up the knife that Chase had bashed from Rebecca's hand.

As he did, Chase realized that it wasn't Agent Stitts either. And yet she recognized the man's handsome face.

It was Frank Carruthers. He'd come back for her.

But as he strode over to Rebecca, who was still holding her side from where Frank had kicked her, Chase began to wonder if the man had come back for her or if he'd come for Rebecca.

To finish the job he started months ago.

Chase, still trying to get her body to react the way she wanted it to, to behave like a good child, scrambled away from Frank who was shouting something incoherent at Rebecca.

He lowered himself to one knee and, as Chase watched, Frank moved the knife in front of her face.

Chase scrambled for her gun and phone under the bed. But before she got there, she noticed something else lying just to the left of her handgun and she hesitated.

It was the syringe, the one that Rebecca had dropped. For what felt like an eternity, Chase remained completely still, on all fours, staring at the syringe, then looking at her badge, her gun, her phone.

"You ruined my life," she heard Frank whisper.

Rebecca tried to reply, but her words came out strangled, much as Chase's had only moments ago.

And then, for some reason, Rebecca started to laugh, a horrible wheezing sound.

Chase realized that she had to make a decision, and she scrambled over to the items under the bed.

With her hand clenched, she propped herself up into a seated position, pressing her back and neck up against the bed frame.

And then she watched as Frank brought the knife ever closer to Rebecca's throat.

"Don't," Chase said. "Don't do it."

But her words were so weak, so lacking in conviction, that she wasn't even sure if Frank had heard her.

Rebecca had, however. She knew this because the woman's eyes darted over at her.

And when she saw what was in Chase's hand, her laughing intensified.

It was a horrible laugh, which transitioned into the bellow of the man in the truck, the one who had taken her sister from her all those years ago, and then combined with the chuckles of all the Johns that she'd had sex with back when she was undercover.

When she needed to please Tyler so that he would feed her the dope she needed.

Chase closed her eyes, and when she opened them, she looked down at herself.

She watched as the syringe made its way to her arm, to the crook of her elbow, seemingly on its own.

Chase didn't feel the needle bite into her skin, maybe because her skin was already scarred, or maybe because she couldn't feel anything in that moment.

"Don't," she whispered, a second before pushing the plunger. "Frank, please don't—take me instead."

Epilogue

"ARE YOU GOING TO be okay to collect your things alone?" The orderly asked, holding the door to the van open for her.

Chase nodded and stepped out into the early morning light. She looked upwards, squinting at the sun that was streaming down on her in thick rays. And yet Chase felt anything but warm.

Nothing could warm the chill that gripped her heart.

She lowered her gaze and stared at the bandage on her left arm and resisted the urge to peel it back and look at the abscess that had formed in the crook of her elbow.

As predicted, a police officer followed her out of the van.

He was a nice guy, if a little on the boring side. And he was polite too, so that when Chase opened her apartment door, he waited outside.

"You going to leave this open?"

The man shrugged.

"Up to you."

Chase nodded and elected to close it. It didn't matter. Even if she was in a physical state capable of running, where would she go?

She looked around the room, which appeared strange to her, as if it wasn't really her room but someone else's. It seemed fake, like a movie set.

Yeah, Chase thought. *That's what this all is. A fucking horror movie.*

Without thinking, she started to rifle clothing, sparse as they were, into the bag that the orderly had handed her.

When she was done, Chase sat on the bed and stared blankly at the wall. She did this for what she thought was a minute, but what could've just as easily been five.

And then she dropped to her knees, lowered her head, and looked beneath the bed.

It was gone.

Chase's breath caught in her throat.

It was all gone.

She straightened and was about to turn around when someone spoke.

"You looking for this?"

A man walked around the bed and stepped in front of Chase, but she was too ashamed to raise her eyes.

"Look at me, Chase."

Chase took a deep breath and then finally looked up.

Stitts was standing in front of her, holding her black leather case in one hand. It was open, and the three bags of heroin stared out at her like the yellow eyes of a cat.

"It's not mine," she said. But the lie was so lame, that Agent Stitts didn't even address it.

"You have a choice to make, Chase."

Chase closed her eyes, envisioning the last things she saw in Leah's neighbor's house: Frank hovering over Rebecca, the knife slowly inching towards her throat.

"What's going to happen to Frank Carruthers, Stitts?"

Agent Stitts pressed his lips together tightly.

"I think it's time that you focused on yourself, Chase. You need help. A lot of help."

For some reason, the comment touched a nerve with Chase, despite everything that had happened.

Her eyes narrowed.

"I passed my psych and medical exams," she spat, realizing that she sounded like a petulant child —*I did my homework now I can watch TV*—but not really caring.

She was beyond caring.

Agents Stitts reached into his shoulder bag and pulled out two folders. He tossed them on the bed beside Chase, and one of them flew open.

From the header, Chase could see that it was her psych exam.

"What the fuck?"

On the top right of the page, written in bold, red type was a single word.

Fail.

Confused, still convinced that this was just a deranged movie set, Chase opened the second folder.

This one contained the results of her medical exam. And, while it didn't have anything written in red, the result under opioids was circled several times.

Tears streamed down her cheeks.

"You did this?"

Stitts nodded.

"I thought that if… if… if you were with me…"

Stitts looked away then, and Chase knew that he too was ashamed. The man had tried to help her, that much was clear; he was always trying to help her, ever since they met back in New York City.

He cared too much, and now he was paying the price.

Stitts cleared his throat before continuing.

"I called Brad and he told me everything. You need help, Chase. But I can't do this for you. You have to make the choice for yourself."

Chase hung her head.

"You can go back to Chicago and face the charges and hope for leniency because you caught Rebecca Hall. But that'll be the end of your career as an FBI agent. Or you can go into rehab—serious rehab, Chase—and hope that with friends in high places, maybe, *just maybe,* one day you can work for the FBI again."

Chase slowly raised her eyes and stared at Agent Stitts's handsome face before answering.

She knew that she had a decision to make.

But what Stitts hadn't told her was that there was a third option.

She could run.

She could run like she had when Georgina had been taken.

Chase could run and never look back.

END

Author's note

I LOVE CHASE ADAMS. Yeah, I said it. Sure, she's got issues, but she never gives up.

Ever.

I hope you're as big a Chase Adams fan as I am. In a few months, she'll be back in the third book in the series, *Drawing Dead*. She has some… umm… issues to deal with first.

Also, in case you didn't know, Chase first appeared in Butterfly Kisses, and also played major roles in Books 2 and 3 in the Detective Damien Drake series. And before you ask, yes, the two will collide again one day.

Maybe soon.

Maybe not so soon.

As always, if you've enjoyed this book, please post a review! And tell your friend (or a cat) about it!

Hit me up on Facebook or via email.

You keep reading, and I'll keep writing.

Patrick
Montreal, 2018

Made in the USA
Columbia, SC
20 December 2023

28942139R00150